DRAW STRAIGHT

DRAW STRAIGHT

A WESTERN SEXTET

Louis L'Amour

Published in 2020 by Blackstone Publishing

Printed in the United States of America

ISBN 978-1-9825-9516-6
Fiction / Westerns

Version 1

Blackstone Publishing
31 Mistletoe Rd.
Ashland, OR 97520

www.BlackstonePublishing.com

DRAW STRAIGHT

CONTENTS

FORK YOUR OWN BRONCS

Mac Marcy turned in the saddle and, resting his left hand on the cantle, glanced back up the arroyo. His lean, brown face was troubled. There were cattle here, all right, but too few.

At this time of day, late afternoon and very hot, there should have been a steady drift of cattle toward the water hole.

Ahead of him he heard a steer bawl and then another. Now what? Above the bawling of the cattle, he heard another sound, a sound that turned his face gray with worry. It was the sound of hammers.

He needed nothing more to tell him what was happening. Jingle Bob Kenyon was fencing the water hole!

As he rounded the bend in the wash, the sound of hammers ceased for an instant, but only for an instant. Then they continued with their work.

Two strands of barbed wire had already been stretched tight and hard across the mouth of the wash. Several cowhands were stretching the third wire of what was obviously to be a four-wire fence.

Already Marcy's cattle were bunching near the fence, bawling for water.

As he rode nearer, two men dropped their hammers and lounged up to the fence. Marcy's eyes narrowed, and his gaze shifted to the big man on the roan horse. Jingle Bob Kenyon was watching him with grim humor.

Marcy avoided the eyes of the two other men by the fence, Vin Ricker and John Soley, who could mean only one thing for him—trouble, bad trouble. Vin Ricker was a gunhand and a killer. John Soley was anything Vin told him to be.

"This is a rotten trick, Kenyon," Marcy declared angrily. "In this heat my herd will be wiped out."

Kenyon's eyes were unrelenting. "That's just tough," he stated flatly. "I warned you when you first come in here to git out while the gittin' was good. You stayed on. You asked for it. Now you take it or git out."

Temper flaring within him like a burst of flame, Marcy glared. But, deliberately, he throttled his fury. He would have no chance here. Ricker and Soley were too much for him, let alone the other hands and Kenyon himself.

"If you don't like it," Ricker sneered, "why don't you stop us? I hear tell you're a plumb salty hombre."

"You'd like me to give you a chance to kill me, wouldn't you?" Marcy asked harshly. "Someday I'll get you without your guns, Ricker, and I'll tear down your meat house."

Ricker laughed. "I don't want to dirty my hands on you, or I'd come over an' make you eat those words. If you ever catch me without these guns, you'll wish to old Harry I still had 'em."

Marcy turned his eyes away from the gunman and looked at Kenyon.

"Kenyon, I didn't think this of you. Without water, my cows won't last three days, and you know it. You'll bust me flat."

Kenyon was unrelenting. "This is a man's country, Marcy," he said dryly. "You fork your own broncs, an' you git your own water. Don't come whinin' to me. You moved in on me, an' if you git along, it'll be on your own."

Kenyon turned his horse and rode away. For an instant Marcy stared after him, seething with rage. Then, abruptly, he wheeled his grayish-black horse—a moros—and started back up the arroyo. Even as he turned, he became aware that only six lean steers faced the barbed wire.

He had ridden but a few yards beyond the bend when that thought struck him like a blow. Six head of all the hundreds he had herded in here. By rights they should all be at the water hole or heading that way. Puzzled, he started back up the trail.

By rights there should be a big herd here. Where could the cattle be? As he rode back toward his claim shack, he stared about him. No cattle were in sight. His range was stripped.

Rustlers? He scowled. But there had been no rustling activity of which he had heard. Ricker and Soley were certainly the type to rustle cattle, but Marcy knew Kenyon had been keeping them busy on the home range.

He rode back toward the shack, his heart heavy.

He had saved for seven years, riding cattle trails to Dodge, Abilene, and Ellsworth to get the money to buy his herd. It was his big chance to have a spread of his own, a chance for some independence and a home.

A home. He stared bitterly at the looming rimrock behind his outfit. A home meant a wife, and there was only one girl in the world for him. There would never be another who could make him feel as Sally Kenyon did. But she would have to be old Jingle Bob's daughter.

Not that she had ever noticed him. But in those first months before the fight with Jingle Bob became dog-eat-dog, Marcy had seen her around, watched her, been in love with her from a distance. He had always hoped that when his place had proved up and he was settled, he might know her better. He might even ask her to marry him.

It had been a foolish dream. Yet day by day, it became even more absurd. He was not only in a fight with her father, but he was closer than ever to being broke.

Grimly, his mind fraught with worry, he cooked his meager supper, crouching before the fireplace. Again and again the thought kept recurring—where were his cattle? If they had been stolen, they would have to be taken down past the water hole and across Jingle Bob's range. There was no other route from Marcy's corner of range against the rim. For a horseman, yes. But not for cattle.

The sound of a walking horse startled him. He straightened, and then stepped away from the fire, and put the bacon upon the plate, listening to the horse as it drew nearer. Then he put down his food, and, loosening his gun, he stepped to the door.

The sun had set long since, but it was not yet dark. He watched a gray horse coming down from the trees leading up to the rim. Suddenly, he gulped in surprise.

It was Sally Kenyon! He stepped outside and walked into the open. The girl saw him and waved a casual hand, and then reined in.

"Have you a drink of water?" she asked, smiling. "It's hot, riding."

"Sure," he said, trying to smile. "Coffee, if you want. I was just fixing to eat a mite. Want to join me? Of course," he said sheepishly, "I ain't no hand with grub."

"I might take some coffee."

Sally swung down, drawing off her gauntlets. She had always seemed a tall girl, but on the ground she came just to his shoulder. Her hair was honey-colored, her eyes gray.

He caught the quick glance of her eyes as she looked around. He saw them hesitate with surprise at the spectacle of flowers blooming near the door. She looked up, and their eyes met.

"Ain't much time to work around," he confessed. "I've sort of been trying to make it look like a home."

"Did you plant the flowers?" she asked curiously.

"Yes, ma'am. My mother was always a great hand for flowers. I like 'em, too, so when I built this cabin, I set some out. The wildflowers, I transplanted."

He poured coffee into a cup and handed it to her. She sipped the hot liquid and looked at him.

"I've been hearing about you," she said.

"From Jingle Bob?"

She nodded. "And some others. Vin Ricker, for one. He hates you."

"Who else?"

"Chen Lee."

"Lee?" Marcy shook his head. "I don't place him."

"He's Chinese, our cook. He seems to know a great deal about you. He thinks you're a fine man. A great fighter, too. He's always talking about some Mullen gang you had trouble with."

"Mullen gang?" He stared. "Why, that was in …" He caught himself. "No, ma'am, I reckon he's mistook. I don't know any Chinese, and there ain't no Mullen gang around I know of."

That, he reflected, was no falsehood. The Mullen gang had all fitted very neatly into the boot hill he had prepared for them back in Bentown. They definitely weren't around.

"Going to stay here?" she asked, looking at him over her coffee cup, her gray eyes level.

His eyes flashed. "I was fixing to, but I reckon your old man has stopped me by fencing that water hole. He's a hard man, your father."

"It's a hard country." She did not smile. "He's got ideas about it. He drove the Mescaleros out. He wiped out the rustlers. He took this range. He doesn't like the idea of any soft-going, second-run cowhand coming in and taking over."

His head jerked up.

"Soft-going?" he flared. "Second-run? Why, that old billy goat."

Sally turned toward her horse. "Don't tell me. Tell him. If you've nerve enough."

He got up and took the bridle of her horse. His eyes were hard.

"Ma'am," he said, striving to make his voice gentle, "I think you're a mighty fine person, and sure enough pretty, but that father of yours is a rough-riding old buzzard. If it wasn't for that Ricker hombre ..."

"Afraid?" she taunted, looking down at him.

"No, ma'am," he said quietly. "Only I ain't a killing man. I was raised a Quaker. I don't aim to do no fighting."

"You're in a fighting man's country," she warned him. "And you are cutting in on a fighting man's range."

She turned her gray and started to ride away. Suddenly, she reined in and looked back over her shoulder.

"By the way," she said, "there's water up on the rim."

Water up on the rim? What did she mean? He turned his head and stared up at the top of the great cliff, which loomed high overhead into the night. It was fully a mile away, but it seemed almost behind his house.

How could he get up to the rim? Sally had come from that direction. In the morning he would try.

In the distance, carried by the still air of night, he heard a cow bawling. It was shut off from the water hole. His six head, starving for water.

Marcy walked out to the corral and threw a saddle on the

moros. He swung into the saddle and rode at a canter toward the water hole.

They heard him coming, and he saw a movement in the shadows by the cottonwoods.

"Hold it!" a voice called. "What do you want?"

"Let that fence down, and put them cows through!" Marcy yelled.

There was a harsh laugh. "Sorry, amigo. No can do. Only Kenyon cows drink here."

"All right," Marcy snapped. "They are Kenyon cows. I'm giving 'em to him. Let the fence down, and let 'em drink. I ain't seeing no animal die just to please an old plug head. Let 'em through."

Then he heard Sally's voice. He saw her sitting her horse beside old Joe Linger, who was her bodyguard, teacher, and friend. An old man who had taught her to ride and to shoot and who had been a scout for the army at some time in the past.

Sally was speaking, and he heard her say: "Let them through, Texas. If they are our cows, we don't want to have them die on us."

Marcy turned the moros and rode back toward his cabin, a sense of defeat heavy upon him …

* * * * *

He rolled out of his blankets with the sun and, after a quick breakfast, saddled the grayish-black horse and started back toward the rim. He kept remembering Sally's words: there is water on the rim. Why had she told him that? What good would water do him if it was way up on the rim?

There must be a way up. By backtracking the girl, he could find it. He was worried about the cattle. The problem of their disappearance kept working into his thoughts. That was another reason for his ride, the major reason. If the cattle were still on his ranch, they were back in the breaks at the foot of the rim.

As he backtracked the girl's horse, he saw cow tracks, more and more of them. Obviously, some of his cattle had drifted this way. It puzzled him, yet he had to admit that he knew little of this country.

Scarcely a year before, he had come into this range, and, when he arrived, the grass in the lower reaches of the valley was good, and there were mesquite beans. The cattle grew fat. With hotter and dryer weather, they had shown more and more of a tendency to keep to shady hillsides and to the canyons.

The cow tracks scattered out and disappeared. He continued on the girl's trail. He was growing more and more puzzled, for he was in the shadow of the great cliff now, and any trail that mounted it must be frightfully steep. Sally, of course, had grown up in this country on horseback. With her always had been Joe Linger. Old Joe had been one of the first white men to settle in the rim country.

Marcy skirted a clump of piñon and emerged on a little sandy level at the foot of the cliff. This, at one distant time, had been a streambed, a steep stream that originated somewhere back up in the rimrock and flowed down here and deeper into his range.

Then he saw the trail. It was a narrow catwalk of rock that clung to the cliff's edge in a way that made him swallow as he looked at it. The catwalk led up the face of the cliff and back into a deep gash in the face of the rim, a gash invisible from below.

The moros snorted a few times, but true to its mountain blood, it took the trail on dainty feet. In an hour Marcy rode out on the rim itself. All was green here, green grass. The foliage on the trees was greener than below. There was every indication of water but no sign of a cow. Not even a range-bred cow would go up such a trail as Marcy had just ridden.

Following the tracks of the gray, Marcy worked back through the cedar and piñon until he began to hear a muffled roar. Then he rode through the trees and reined in at the edge of a pool that was some twenty feet across. Water flowed into it from a fair-size stream, bubbling over rocks and falling into the pool. There were a number of springs here, and undoubtedly the supply of water was limitless. But where did it go?

Dismounting, Marcy walked down to the edge of the water and knelt on a flat rock and leaned far out.

Brush hung far out over the water at the end of the pool, brush that grew on a rocky ledge no more than three feet above the surface of the water. But beneath that ledge was a black hole at least eight feet long. Water from the pool was pouring into that black hole.

Mac Marcy got up and walked around the pool to the ledge. The brush was very thick, and he had to force his way through. Clinging precariously to a clump of manzanita, he leaned out over the rim of the ledge and tried to peer into the hole. He could see nothing except a black slope of water and that the water fell steeply beyond that slope.

He leaned farther out, felt the manzanita give way slowly, and made a wild clutch at the neighboring brush. Then he plunged into the icy waters of the pool.

He felt himself going down, down, down! He struck out, trying to swim, but the current caught him and swept him into the gaping mouth of the wide black hole under the ledge.

Darkness closed over his head. He felt himself shooting downward. He struck something and felt it give beneath him, and then something hit him a powerful blow on the head. Blackness and icy water closed over him.

* * * * *

Chattering teeth awakened him. He was chilled to the bone and soaking wet. For a moment he lay on hard, smooth rock in darkness, head throbbing, trying to realize what had happened. His feet felt cold. He pulled them up and turned over to a sitting position in a large cave. Only then did he realize his feet had been lying in a pool of water.

Far above he could see a faint glimmer of light, a glimmer feebly reflecting from the black, glistening roar of a fall. He tilted his head back and stared upward through the gloom. That dim light, the hole through which he had come, was at least sixty feet above him!

In falling he had struck some obstruction in the narrow chimney of the water's course, some piece of driftwood or brush insecurely wedged across the hole. It had broken his descent and had saved him.

His matches would be useless. Feeling around the cave floor in the dark, he found some dry tinder that had been lying here for years. He still had his guns, since they had been tied in place with rawhide thongs. He drew one of them, extracted a cartridge, and went to work on it with his hunting knife.

When it was open, he placed it carefully on the rock beside him. Then he cut shavings and crushed dried bark in his hand. Atop this he placed the powder from the open cartridge.

Then he went to work to strike a spark from a rock with the steel back of his knife. There was not the slightest wind here. Despite that, he worked for the better part of an hour before a spark sprang into the powder.

There was a bright burst of flame, and the shavings crackled. He added fuel and then straightened up and stepped back to look around.

He stood on a wide ledge in the gloomy, closed cavern at the foot of the fall's first drop, down which he had fallen. The water struck the rock not ten feet away from him. Then it took another steep drop off to the left. He could see by the driftwood that had fallen clear that it was the usual thing for the rushing water to cast all waterborne objects onto this ledge.

The ledge had at one time been deeply gouged and worn by running water. Picking up a torch, Marcy turned and glanced away into the darkness. There lay the old dry channel, deeply worn and polished by former running water.

At some time in the past, this had been the route of the stream underground. In an earthquake or some breakthrough of the rock, the water had taken the new course.

Thoughtfully, Marcy calculated his situation. He was fearful of his predicament. From the first moment of consciousness in that utter darkness, he had been so. There is no fear more universal than the fear of entombment alive, the fear of choking, strangling in utter darkness beyond the reach of help.

Mac Marcy was no fool. He was, he knew, beyond the reach of help. The moros was ground-hitched in a spot where there was plenty of grass and water. The grayish-black horse would stay right there.

No one, with the exception of Sally, ever went to the top of the rim. It was highly improbable that she would go again soon. In many cases, weeks would go by without anyone stopping by Marcy's lonely cabin. If he was going to get out of this hole, he would have to do it by his own efforts.

One glance up that fall showed him there was no chance of going back up the way he had come down. Working his way over to the next step downward of the fall, he held out his torch and peered below. All was utter blackness, with only the cold damp of falling water in the air.

Fear was mounting within him now, but he fought it back, forcing himself to be calm and to think carefully. The old dry channel remained a vague hope. But, to all appearances, it went deeper and deeper into the stygian blackness of the earth. He put more fuel on his fire and started exploring again. Fortunately, the wood he was burning was bone dry and made almost no smoke.

Torch in hand, he started down the old dry channel. This had been a watercourse for many, many years. The rock was worn and polished. He had gone no more than sixty feet when the channel divided.

On the left was a black, forbidding hole, scarcely waist high. Down that route most of the water seemed to have gone, as it was worn the deepest.

On the right was an opening almost like a doorway. Marcy stepped over to it and held his torch out. It also was a black hole. He had a sensation of awful depth. Stepping back, he picked up a rock. Leaning out, he dropped it into the hole on the right.

For a long time, he listened. Then, somewhere far below, there was a splash. This hole was literally hundreds of feet deep. It would end far below the level of the land on which his cabin stood.

He drew back. Sweat stood out on his forehead, and, when he put his hand to it, his brow felt cold and clammy. He looked at the black waist-high hole on the left and felt fear rise within him as he had never felt it before. He drew back and wet his lips.

His torch was almost burned out. Turning with the last of its light, he retraced his steps to the ledge by the fall.

How long he had been below ground, he didn't know. He looked up, and there was still a feeble light from above. But it seemed to have grown less. Had night almost come?

Slowly, he built a new torch. This was his last chance of escape. It was a chance he had already begun to give up. Of them all, that black hole on the left was least promising, but he must explore it.

He pulled his hat down a little tighter and started back to

where the tunnel divided into two holes. His jaw was set grimly. He got down on his hands and knees and edged into the black hole on the left.

Once inside, he found it fell away steeply in a mass of loose boulders. Scrambling over them, he came to a straight, steep fall of at least ten feet. Glancing at the sheer drop, he knew one thing—once down there, he would never get back up.

Holding his torch high, he looked beyond. Nothing but darkness. Behind him there was no hope. He hesitated and then got down on his hands and knees, lowered himself over the edge, and dropped ten feet.

This time he had to be right, for there was no going back. He walked down a slanting tunnel. It seemed to be growing darker. Glancing up at his torch, he saw it was burning out. In a matter of minutes, he would be in total darkness.

He walked faster and faster. Then he broke into a stumbling run, fear rising within him. Something brought him up short, and for a moment he did not see what had caused him to halt in his blind rush. Then hope broke over him like a cold shower of rain.

There on the sand beneath his feet were tiny tracks. He bent over them. A pack rat or some other tiny creature. Getting up, he hurried on, and, seeing a faint glow ahead, he rushed around a bend. There before him was the feeble glow of the fading day. His torch guttered and went out.

He walked on to the cave mouth, trembling in every limb. Mac Marcy was standing in an old watercourse that came out from behind some boulders not two miles from his cabin.

He stumbled home and fell into his bunk, almost too tired to undress.

* * * * *

Marcy awakened to a frantic pounding on his door. Staggering erect, he pulled on his boots, yelling out as he did so. Then he drew on his Levi's and shirt and opened the door, buttoning his shirt with one hand.

Sally, her face deathly pale, was standing outside. Beyond her gray mare stood Marcy's moros. At the sight of him, the grayish-black horse lifted his head and pricked up his ears.

"Oh," Sally gasped. "I thought you were dead … drowned."

He stepped over beside her.

"No," he said, "I guess I'm still here. You're pretty scared, ma'am. What's there for you to be scared about?"

"Why," she burst out impatiently, "if you …" She caught herself and stopped abruptly. "After all," she continued coolly, "no one wants to find a friend drowned."

"Ma'am," he said sincerely, "if you get that wrought up, I'll get myself almost drowned every day."

She stared at him and then smiled. "I think you're a fool," she said. She mounted and turned. "But a nice fool."

Marcy stared after her thoughtfully. Well now, maybe …

He glanced down at his boots. Where they had lain in the pool, there was water-stain on them. Also, there was a small green leaf clinging to the rough leather. He stooped and picked it off, wadded it up, and started to throw it away when he was struck by an idea. He unfolded the leaf and studied the veins. Suddenly, his face broke into a grin.

"Boy," he said to the moros, "we got us a job to do, even if you do need a rest." He swung into the saddle and rode back toward the watercourse, still grinning.

* * * * *

It was midafternoon when he returned to the cabin and ate a leisurely lunch, still chuckling. Then he mounted again and started for the old water hole that had been fenced by Jingle Bob Kenyon.

When Marcy rounded the bend, he could see that something was wrong. A dozen men were gathered around the water hole. Nearby and astride her gray was Sally.

The men were in serious conference, and they did not notice Marcy's approach. He rode up, leaning on the horn of the saddle, and watched them, smiling.

Suddenly, Vin Ricker looked up. His face went hard.

Mac Marcy swung down and strolled up to the fence, leaning casually on a post.

"What's up?"

"The water hole's gone dry!" Kenyon exploded. "Not a drop o' water in it."

Smothering a grin, Marcy rolled a smoke.

"Well," he said philosophically, "the Lord giveth and He taketh away. No doubt it's the curse of the Lord for your greed, Jingle Bob."

Kenyon glared at him suspiciously. "You know somethin' about this?" he demanded. "Man, in this hot weather my cattle will die by the hundreds. Somethin's got to be done."

"Seems to me," Marcy said dryly, "I have heard those words before."

Sally was looking at him over her father's head, her face grave and questioning. But she said nothing, gave no sign of approval or disapproval.

"This here's a man's country," Marcy said seriously. "You fork your own broncs, and you get your own water."

Kenyon flushed. "Marcy, if you know anythin' about this, for goodness sake, spill it. My cows will die. Maybe I was too stiff about this, but there's somethin' mighty funny goin' on here. This water hole ain't failed in twenty years."

"Let me handle him," Ricker snarled. "I'm just achin' to git my hands on him."

"Don't ache too hard, or you'll git your wish," Marcy drawled, and he crawled through the fence. "All right, Kenyon, we'll talk business," Marcy said to the rancher. "You had me stuck yesterday with my tail in a crack. Now you got yours in one. I cut off your water to teach you a lesson. You're a blamed old highbinder, and it's high time you had some teeth pulled.

"Nobody but me knows how that water's cut off and where. If I don't change it, nobody can. So listen to what I'm saying. I'm going to have all the water I need after this on my own place, but this here hole stays open. No fences.

"This morning, when I went up to cut off your water, I saw some cow tracks. I'm missing a powerful lot of cows. I followed the tracks into a hidden draw and found three hundred of my cattle and about a hundred head of yours, all nicely corralled and ready to be herded across the border.

"While I was looking over the hideout, I spied Ricker there. John Soley then came riding up with about thirty head of your cattle, and they run 'em in with the rest."

"You're a liar!" Ricker burst out, his face tense, and he dropped into a crouch, his fingers spread.

Marcy was unmoved. "No, I ain't bluffing. You try to prove where you were about nine this morning. And don't go trying to get me into a gunfight. I ain't a-going to draw, and you don't dare shoot me down in front of witnesses. But you take off those guns, and I'll …"

Ricker's face was ugly. "You bet I'll take 'em off! I allus did want a crack at that purty face o' yours."

He stripped off his guns and swung them to Soley in one movement. Then he rushed.

A wicked right swing caught Marcy before he dropped his gun belt and got his hands up, and it knocked him reeling into the dirt.

Ricker charged, his face livid, trying to kick Marcy with his boots, but Marcy rolled over and got on his feet. He lunged and swung a right that clipped Ricker on the temple. Then Marcy stabbed the rustler with a long left. They started to slug.

Neither had any knowledge of science. Both were raw and tough and hard-bitten. Toe to toe, bloody and bitter, they slugged it out. Ricker, confident and the larger of the two men, rushed in swinging. One of his swings cut Marcy's eye; another started blood gushing from Marcy's nose. Ricker set himself and threw a hard right for Marcy's chin, but the punch missed as Marcy swung one to the body that staggered Ricker.

They came in again, and Marcy's big fist pulped the rustler's lips, smashing him back on his heels. Then Marcy followed it in, swinging with both hands. His breath came in great gasps, but his eyes were blazing. He charged in, following Ricker relentlessly.

Suddenly, Marcy's right caught the gunman and knocked him to his knees. Marcy stepped back and let him get up, and then knocked him sliding on his face in the sand. Ricker tried to get up, but he fell back, bloody and beaten.

Swiftly, before the slow-thinking Soley realized what was happening, Marcy spun and grabbed one of his own guns and turned it on this rustler.

"Drop 'em," he snapped. "Unbuckle your belt, and step back."

Jingle Bob Kenyon leaned on his saddle horn, chewing his pipe stem thoughtfully.

"What," he drawled, "would you have done if he drawed his gun?"

Marcy looked up, surprised. "Why, I'd have killed him, of course." He glanced over at Sally and then looked back at

Kenyon. "Before we get off the subject," he said, "we finish our deal. I'll turn your water back into this hole … I got it stopped up away back inside the mountain … but, as I said, the hole stays open to anybody. Also …" Marcy's face colored a little. "I'm marrying Sally."

"You're what?" Kenyon glared, and then jerked around to look at his daughter.

Sally's eyes were bright. "You heard him, Father," she replied coolly. "I'm taking back with me those six steers he gave you so he can get them to water."

Marcy was looking at Kenyon when suddenly Marcy grinned.

"I reckon," he said, "you had your lesson. Sally and me have got a lot of talking to do."

Marcy swung aboard the moros, and he and Sally started off together.

Jingle Bob Kenyon stared after them, grim humor in his eyes.

"I wonder," he said, "what he would have done if Ricker had drawed?"

Old Joe Linger grinned and looked over at Kenyon from under his bushy brows. "Jest what he said. He'd've kilt him. That's Quaker John McMarcy, the hombre that wiped out the Mullen gang single-handed. He jest don't like to fight, that's all."

"It sure does beat all," Kenyon said thoughtfully. "The trouble a man has to go to git him a good son-in-law these days."

KEEP TRAVELIN', RIDER

I

When Tack Gentry sighted the weather-beaten buildings of the G Bar, he touched spurs to the buckskin, and the horse broke into a fast canter that carried the cowhand down the trail and around into the ranch yard. He swung down.

"Hey!" he yelled happily, grinning. "Is that all the welcome I get?"

The door pushed open, and a man stepped out on the worn porch. The man had a stubble of beard and a drooping mustache. His blue eyes were small and narrow.

"Who are you?" he demanded. "And what do you want?"

"I'm Tack Gentry," Tack said. "Where's Uncle John?"

"I don't know you," the man said, "and I never heard of no Uncle John. I reckon you got onto the wrong spread, youngster."

"Wrong spread?" Tack laughed. "Quit your funnin'! I helped build that house there, and built the corrals by my lonesome while Uncle John was sick. Where is everybody?"

The man looked at him carefully and then lifted his eyes to a point beyond Tack. A voice spoke from behind the cowhand. "Reckon you been gone a while, ain't you?"

Gentry turned. The man behind him was short, stocky, and blond. He had a wide, flat face, a small broken nose, and cruel eyes.

"Gone? I reckon, yes. I've been gone most of a year. Went north with a trail herd to Ellsworth, then took me a job as *segundo* on a herd movin' to Wyoming."

Tack stared around, his eyes alert and curious. There was something wrong here, something very wrong. The neatness that had been typical of Uncle John Gentry was gone. The place looked run-down, the porch was untidy, the door hung loosely on its hinges, even the horses in the corral were different.

"Where's Uncle John?" Tack demanded again. "Quit stallin'!"

The blond man smiled, his lips parting over broken teeth and a hard, cynical light coming into his eyes. "If you mean John Gentry, who used to live on this place, he's gone. He drawed on the wrong man and got himself killed."

"What?" Tack's stomach felt like he had been kicked. He stood there, staring. "He *drew* on somebody? Uncle John?" Tack shook his head. "That's impossible. John Gentry was a Quaker. He never lifted a hand in violence against anybody or anything in his life. He never even wore a gun, never owned one."

"I only know what they tell me," the blond man said, "but we got work to do, and I reckon you better slope out of here. And," he added grimly, "if you're smart, you'll keep right on goin', clean out of the country!"

"What do you mean?" Tack's thoughts were in a turmoil, trying to accustom himself to this change, wondering what could have happened, what was behind it.

"I mean you'll find things considerably changed around here. If you decide not to leave," he added, "you might ride into Sunbonnet and look up Van Hardin or Dick Olney, and tell him I said to give you all you had comin'. Tell 'em Soderman sent you."

"Who's Van Hardin?" Tack asked. The name was unfamiliar.

"You been away, all right," Soderman acknowledged, "or you'd know who Van Hardin is. He runs this country. He's the ramrod, Hardin is. Olney's sheriff."

* * * * *

Tack Gentry rode away from his home ranch with his thoughts in confusion. Uncle John killed in a gunfight? Why, that was out of reason! The old man wouldn't fight. He never had and never would. And this Dick Olney was sheriff! What had become of Pete Liscomb? No election was due for another year, and Pete had been a good sheriff.

There was one way to solve the problem and get the whole story, and that was to circle around and ride by the London Ranch. Bill could give him the whole story, and, besides, he wanted to see Betty. It had been a long time.

The six miles to the headquarters of the London Ranch went by swiftly, yet as Tack rode, he scanned the grassy levels along the Maravillas. There were cattle enough, more than he had ever seen on the old G Bar, and all of them wearing the G Bar brand.

He reined in sharply. What the . . . ? Why, if Uncle John was dead, the ranch belonged to him! But if that was so, who was Soderman? And what were they doing on his ranch?

Three men were loafing on the wide verandah of the London ranch house when Tack rode up. All their faces were unfamiliar. He glanced warily from one to the other.

"Where's Bill London?" he asked.

"London?" The man in the wide brown hat shrugged. "Reckon he's to home, over in Sunbonnet Pass. He ain't never over here."

"This is his ranch, isn't it?" Tack demanded.

All three men seemed to tense. "His ranch?" The man in the brown hat shook his head. "Reckon you're a stranger around here. This ranch belongs to Van Hardin. London ain't got a ranch. Nothin' but a few acres back against the creek over to Sunbonnet Pass. He and that girl of his live there. I reckon, though . . ." He grinned suddenly. ". . . She won't be there much longer. Hear tell she's goin' to work in the Longhorn dance hall."

"Betty London? In the Longhorn?" Tack exclaimed. "Don't make me laugh, partner! Betty's too nice a girl for that! She wouldn't . . ."

"They got it advertised," the brown-hatted man said calmly.

* * * * *

An hour later a very thoughtful Tack Gentry rode up the dusty street of Sunbonnet. In that hour of riding, he had been doing a lot of thinking, and he was remembering what Soderman had said. He was to tell Hardin or Olney that Soderman had sent him to get all that was coming to him. Suddenly, that remark took on a new significance.

Tack swung down in front of the Longhorn. Emblazoned on the front of the saloon was a huge poster announcing that Betty London was the coming attraction, that she would sing and entertain at the Longhorn. Compressing his lips, Tack walked into the saloon.

Nothing was familiar except the bar and the tables. The man behind the bar was squat and fat, and his eyes peered at Tack from folds of flesh. "What's it fur you?" he demanded.

"Rye," Tack said. He let his eyes swing slowly around the room. Not a familiar face greeted him. Shorty Davis was gone. Nick Farmer was not around. These men were strangers, a tight-mouthed, hard-eyed crew.

Gentry glanced at the bartender. "Any ridin' jobs around here? Driftin' through, and thought I might like to tie in with one of the outfits around here."

"Keep driftin'," the bartender said, not glancing at him. "Everybody's got a full crew."

One door swung open, and a tall, clean-cut man walked into the room, glancing around. He wore a neat gray suit and a dark hat. Tack saw the bartender's eyes harden and glanced thoughtfully at the newcomer. The man's face was very thin, and, when he removed his hat, his ash blond hair was neatly combed.

He glanced around, and his eyes lighted on Tack. "Stranger?" he asked pleasantly. "Then may I buy you a drink? I don't like to drink alone but haven't sunk so low as to drink with these coyotes."

Tack stiffened, expecting a reaction from some of the seated men, but there was none. Puzzled, he glanced at the blond man and, seeing the cynical good humor in the man's eyes, nodded. "Sure, I'll drink with you."

"My name," the tall man added, "is Anson Childe, by profession a lawyer, by dint of circumstances a gambler, and by choice a student. You perhaps wonder," he added, "why these men do not resent my reference to them as coyotes. There are three reasons, I expect. The first is that some subconscious sense of truth makes them appreciate the justice of the term. Second, they know I am gifted with considerable dexterity in expounding the gospel of Judge Colt. Third, they know that I am dying of tuberculosis and as a result have no fear of bullets. It is not exactly fear that keeps them from drawing on me. Let us say it is a matter of mathematics, and a problem none of them has succeeded in solving with any degree of comfort is the result. It is ... how many of them would die before I did? You can appreciate, my friend, the quandary in which this places them, and also the disagreeable realization that bullets are no respecters of persons, nor am I. The several out there who might draw know that I know who they are. The result is that they know they would be first to die." Childe looked at Tack thoughtfully. "I heard you ask about a riding job as I came in. You look like an honest man, and there is no place here for such."

Gentry hunted for the right words. Then he said: "This country looks like it was settled by honest men."

Anson Childe studied his glass. "Yes," he said, "but at the right moment, they lacked a leader. One was too opposed to violence, another was too law-abiding, and the rest lacked resolution."

If there was a friend in the community, this man was it. Tack finished his drink and strode to the door. The bartender met his eyes as he glanced back.

"Keep on driftin'," the bartender said.

Tack Gentry smiled. "I like it here," he said, "and I'm stayin'."

He swung into the saddle and turned his buckskin toward Sunbonnet Pass. He still had no idea exactly what had happened during the year of his absence, yet Childe's remark coupled with what the others had said told him a little. Apparently some strong, resolute men had moved in and taken over, and there had been no concerted fight against them, no organization, and no leadership.

Childe had said that one was opposed to violence. That would have been his Uncle John. The one who was too law-abiding would be Bill London. London had always been strong for law and order and settling things in a legal way. The others had been honest men but small ranchers, and individually unable to oppose whatever was done to them. Yet whatever had happened, the incoming elements had apparently moved with speed and finesse. Had it been one ranch, it would have been different. But the ranches and the town seemed completely subjugated.

* * * * *

The buckskin took the trail at an easy canter, skirting the long red cliff of Horse Thief Mesa and wading the creek at Gunsight. Sunbonnet Pass opened before him like a gate in the mountains. To the left, in a grove of trees, was a small adobe house and a corral.

Two horses were standing at the corral as he rode up. His eyes narrowed as he saw them. Button and Blackie! Two of his uncle's favorites and two horses he had raised from colts. He swung down and started toward them, when he saw the three people on the steps.

He turned to face them, and his heart jumped. Betty London had not changed.

Her eyes widened, and her face went dead white. "Tack!" she gasped. "Tack Gentry!"

Even as she spoke, Tack saw the sudden shock with which the two men turned to stare. "That's right, Betty," he said quietly. "I just got home."

"But … but … we heard you were dead!"

"I'm not." His eyes shifted to the two men—a thick-shouldered, deep-chested man with a square, swarthy face and a lean, rawboned man wearing a star. The one with the star would be Dick Olney. The other must be Van Hardin.

Tack's eyes swung to Olney. "I heard my uncle, John Gentry, was killed. Did you investigate his death?"

Olney's eyes were careful. "Yeah," he said. "He was killed in a fair fight. Gun in his hand."

"My uncle," Tack replied, "was a Quaker. He never lifted a hand in violence in his life."

"He was a might slow, I reckon," Olney said coolly, "but he had the gun in his hand when I found him."

"Who shot him?"

"Hombre name of Soderman. But like I say, it was a fair fight."

"Like blazes!" Tack flashed. "You'll never make me believe Uncle John wore a gun! That gun was planted on him!"

"You're jumpin' to conclusions," Van Hardin said smoothly. "I saw the gun myself. There were a dozen witnesses."

"Who saw the fight?" Gentry demanded.

"They saw the gun in his hand. In his right hand," Hardin said.

Tack laughed suddenly, harshly. "That does it. Uncle John's right hand has been useless ever since Shiloh, when it was shot to pieces tryin' to get to a wounded soldier. He couldn't hold a feather in those fingers, let alone a gun."

Hardin's face tightened, and Dick Olney's eyes shifted to Hardin's face.

"You'd be better off," Hardin said quietly, "to let sleepin' dogs lie. We ain't goin' to have you comin' in here stirrin' up a peaceful community."

"My uncle John was murdered," Gentry said quietly. "I mean to see his murderer punished. That ranch belongs to me. I intend to get it back."

Van Hardin smiled. "Evidently, you aren't aware of what happened here," he said quietly. "Your uncle was in a noncom-batant outfit durin' the war, was he not? Well, while he was gone, the ranch he had claimed was abandoned. Soderman and I started to run cattle on that range and the land that was claimed by Bill London. No claim to the range was asserted by anyone. We made improvements, and then, durin' our temporary absence with a trail herd, John Gentry and Bill London returned and moved in. Naturally, when we returned, the case was taken to court. The court ruled the ranches belonged to Soderman and myself."

"And the cattle?" Tack asked. "What of the cattle my uncle owned?"

Hardin shrugged. "The brand had been taken over by the new owners and registered in their name. As I understand it, you left with a trail herd immediately after you came back to Texas. My claim was originally asserted during your uncle's absence. I could," he smiled, "lay claim to the money you got from that trail herd. Where is it?"

"Suppose you find out?" Tack replied. "I'm goin' to tell you one thing. I'm goin' to find who murdered my uncle, if it was Soderman or not. I'm also goin' to fight you in court. Now, if you'll excuse me," he turned his eyes to Betty, who had stood, wide-eyed and silent, "I'd like to talk to Bill London."

"He can't see you," Hardin said. "He's asleep."

Gentry's eyes hardened. "You runnin' this place, too?"

"Betty London is going to work for me," Hardin replied. "We may be married later, so in a sense I'm speaking for her."

"Is that right?" Tack demanded, his eyes meeting Betty's.

Her face was miserable. "I'm afraid it is, Tack."

"You've forgotten your promise, then?" he demanded.

"Things . . . things changed, Tack," she faltered. "I . . . I can't talk about it."

"I reckon, Gentry," Olney interrupted, "it's time you rode on. There's nothin' in this neck of the woods for you. You've played out your hand here. Ride on, and you'll save yourself a lot of trouble. They're hirin' hands over on the Pecos."

"I'm stayin," Gentry said flatly.

"Remember," Olney warned, "I'm the sheriff. At the first sign of trouble, I'll come lookin' for you."

Gentry swung into the saddle. His eyes shifted to Betty's face, and for an instant she seemed about to speak. Then he turned and rode away. He did not look back. It was not until after he was gone that he remembered Button and Blackie. To think they were in the possession of Hardin and Olney! The twin blacks he had reared and worked with, training them to do tricks, teaching them all the lore of the cow country horses and much more.

The picture was clear now. In the year in which he had been gone, these men had come in, asserted their claims, taken them to carpetbag courts, and made them stick. Backing their legal claims with guns, they had taken over the country with speed and finesse. At every turn, he was blocked. Betty had turned against him. Bill London was either a prisoner in his own house or something else was wrong. Olney was sheriff, and probably they had their own judge.

He could quit. He could pull out and go on to the Pecos. It would be the easiest way. It was even what Uncle John might have wished him to do, for John Gentry was a peace-loving man. Tack Gentry was of another breed. His father had been killed fighting Comanches, and Tack had gone to war when a mere boy. Uncle John had found a place for himself in a noncombatant outfit, but Tack had fought long and well.

His ride north with the trail herd had been rough and bloody. Twice they had fought off Indians, and once they had mixed it with rustlers. In Ellsworth, a gunman named Paris had made trouble that ended with Paris dead on the floor. Tack had left town in a hurry, ridden to the new camp at Dodge, and then joined a trail herd headed for Wyoming. Indian fighting had been the order of the day, and once, rounding up a bunch of steers lost from the herd in a stampede, Tack had run into three rustlers after the same steers. Tack had downed two of them in the subsequent battle, and then shot it out with the other in a day-long rifle battle that covered a cedar- and boulder-strewn hillside. Finally, just before sundown, they met in a hand-to-hand battle with Bowie knives.

Tack remained long enough to see his old friend Major Powell, with whom he had participated in the Wagon Box fight, and then had wandered back to Kansas. On the Platte he had joined a bunch of buffalo hunters, stayed with them a couple of months, and then trailed back to Dodge.

II

Sunbonnet's Longhorn Saloon was ablaze with lights when he drifted into town that night. He stopped at the livery stable and put up his horse. He had taken a roundabout route, scouting the country, so he decided that Hardin and Olney were probably already in town. By now they would know of his call at the ranch and his meeting with Anson Childe.

He was laboring under no delusions about his future. Van Hardin would not hesitate to see him put out of the way if he attempted to regain his property. Hardin had brains, and Olney was no fool. There were things Gentry must know before anything could be done, and the one man in town who could and would tell him was Childe.

Leaving the livery stable, he started up the street. Turning, he glanced back to see the liveryman standing in the stable door. He dropped his hand quickly, but Gentry believed he had signaled someone across the street. Yet there was no one in sight, and the row of buildings seemed blank and empty.

Only three buildings were lighted. The Longhorn, a smaller, cheaper saloon, and the old general store. There was a light upstairs over the small saloon and several lights in the annex to the Longhorn, which passed as a hotel, the only one in Sunbonnet.

Tack walked along the street, his bootheels sounding loud in the still night air. Ahead of him was a space between the buildings, and when he drew abreast of it, he did a quick sidestep off the street, flattening against the building.

He heard footsteps, hesitation, and then lightly running steps, and suddenly a man dived around the corner and grated to a stop on the gravel, staring down the alleyway between the buildings. He did not see Tack, who was flattened in the dense shadow against the building and behind a rain barrel.

The man started forward suddenly, and Tack reached out and grabbed his ankle. Caught in mid-stride, the fellow plunged over on his head and then lay still. For an instant Gentry hesitated, then struck and shielded a match with his left hand. It was the brown-hatted man he had talked to on the porch of London's ranch. His head had hit a stone, and he was out cold.

Swiftly, Tack shucked the fellow's gun and emptied the shells from it and then pushed it back in his holster. A folded paper had fallen from the unconscious man's pocket, and Tack picked it up. Then, moving fast, he went down the alley until he was in back of the small saloon. By the light from a back window, he read the note.

"This," he muttered, "may help."

> Come to town quick. Trouble's brewing. We can't have anything happen now.
>
> V.H.

Van Hardin. They didn't want trouble now. Why *now?* Folding the note, he slipped it into his pocket and flattened against the side of the saloon, studying the interior. Only two men sat in the dim interior, two men who played cards at a small table. The bartender leaned on the bar and read a newspaper. When the bartender turned his head, Tack recognized him.

Red Furness had worked for his father. He had soldiered with him. He might still be friendly. Tack lifted his knuckles and tapped lightly on the window.

At the second tap, Red looked up. Tack lighted a match and moved it past the window. Neither of the card players seemed to have noticed. Red straightened, folded his paper, and then, picking up a cup, walked back toward the window. When he got there, he dipped the cup into the water bucket with one hand and with the other lifted the window a few inches.

"This is Tack Gentry. Where does Childe hang out?"

Red's whisper was low. "Got him an office and sleepin' room upstairs. There's a back stairway. You watch yourself."

Tack stepped away from his window and made his way to the stairway he had already glimpsed. It might be a trap, but he believed Red was loyal. Also, he was not sure the word was out to kill him. They probably merely wanted him out of the way and hoped he could be warned to move on. The position of the Hardin group seemed secure enough.

Reaching the top of the stairs, he walked along the narrow catwalk to the door. He tapped softly. After an instant, there was a voice. "What do you want?"

"This is Tack Gentry. You talked to me in the saloon." The door opened to darkness, and he stepped in. When it closed, he felt a pistol barrel against his spine.

"Hold still," Childe warned.

Behind him a match struck, and then a candle was lighted. The light still glowed in the other room, seen only by the crack under the door. Childe grinned at him. "Got to be careful," he said. "They have tried twice to dry-gulch me. I put flowers on their graves every Monday." He smiled. "And keep an extra one dug. Ever since I had that new grave dug, I've been left alone. Somehow it seems to have a very sobering influence on the local roughs." He sat down. "I tire quicker than I once did. So you're Gentry. Betty London told me about you. She thought you were dead. There was a rumor that you'd been killed by the Indians in Wyoming."

"No, I came out all right. What I want to know, rememberin' you said you were a lawyer, is what kind of a claim do they have on my ranch?"

"A good one, unfortunately. While you and your uncle were gone … and most of the other men in the locality … several of these men came in and began to brand cattle. After branding a good many, they left. They returned and began working around, about the time you left, and then they ordered your uncle off. He wouldn't go, and they took the case to court. There were no lawyers here then, and your uncle tried to handle it himself. The judge was their man, and suddenly a half dozen witnesses appeared and were sworn in. They testified that the land had been taken and held by Soderman, Olney, and Hardin. They claimed their brands on the cattle asserted their claim to the land, to the home ranches of both London and Gentry. The free range was something else, but with the two big ranches in their hands and the bulk of the free range lying beyond their holdings, they were in a position to freeze out the smaller ranchers. They established a squatter's right to each of the big ranches."

"Can they do that?" Tack demanded. "It doesn't seem fair."

"The usual thing is to allow no claim unless they have occupied the land for twenty years without hindrance, but with a carpetbag court, they do about as they please. Judge Weaver is completely in Van Hardin's hands, and your uncle was on the losing side in this war."

"How did Uncle John get killed?" Tack asked.

Childe shrugged. "They said he called Soderman a liar, and Soderman went for his gun. Your uncle had a gun on him when they found him. It was probably a cold-blooded killing, because Gentry planned on a trip to Austin and was going to appeal the case."

"Have you seen Bill London lately?"

"Only once since the accident."

"Accident?"

"Yes, London was headed for home, dozing along in the buckboard as he always did, when his team ran away with him. The buckboard was overturned, and London's back was injured. He can't ride anymore and can't sit up very long at a time."

"Was it really an accident?" Tack wanted to know.

Childe shrugged. "I doubt it. We couldn't prove a thing. One of the horses had a bad cut on the hip. It looked as if someone with a steel-tipped bullwhip had hit the animal from beside the road."

"Thorough," Tack said. "They don't miss a bet."

Childe nodded. Leaning back in his chair, he put his feet on the desk. He studied Tack Gentry thoughtfully. "You know, you'll be next. They won't stand for you messing around. I think you already have them worried."

Tack explained about the man following him and then handed the note to Childe. The lawyer's eyes narrowed. "Hmm, sounds like they had some reason to soft-pedal the whole thing for a while. Maybe it's an idea for us. Maybe somebody is coming down here to look around, or maybe somebody has grown suspicious."

Tack looked at Childe thoughtfully. "What's your position in all this?"

The tall man shrugged and then laughed lightly. "I've no stake in it, Gentry. I didn't know London, or your uncle, either.

But I heard rumors, and I didn't like the attitude of the local bosses, Hardin and Olney. I'm just a burr under the saddle with which they ride this community, no more. It amuses me to needle them, and they are afraid of me."

"Got any clients?"

"Clients?" Anson Childe chuckled. "Not a one. Not likely to have any, either. In a country so throttled by one man as this is, there isn't any litigation. Nobody can win against him, and they are too busy hating Hardin to want to have trouble with each other."

"Well, then," Tack said, "you've got a client now. Go down to Austin. Demand an investigation. Lay the facts on the table for them. Maybe you can't do any good, but at least you can stir up a lot of trouble. The main thing will be to get people talking. They evidently want quiet, so we'll give them noise. Find out all you can. Get some detectives started on Hardin's trail. Find out who they are, who they were, and where they came from."

Childe sat up. "I'd like it," he said ruefully, "but I don't have that kind of money." He gestured at the room. "I'm behind on my rent here. Red owns the building, so he lets me stay."

Tack grinned and unbuttoned his shirt, drawing out a money belt. "I sold some cattle up north." He counted out a thousand dollars. "Take that. Spend all or any part of it, but create a smell down there. Tell everybody about the situation here."

Childe got up, his face flushed with enthusiasm. "Man, nothing could please me more. I'll make it hot for them. I'll . . ." He went into a fit of coughing, and Tack watched him gravely. Finally, Childe straightened. "You're putting your trust in a sick man, Gentry."

"I'm putting my trust in a fighter," Tack said dryly. "You'll do." He hesitated briefly. "Also, check the title on this land."

They shook hands silently, and Tack went to the door. Softly he opened it and stepped out into the cool night. Well, for better or worse, the battle was opened now for the next step. He came down off the wooden stairs and then walked to the street. There was no one in sight. Tack Gentry crossed the street and pushed through the swinging doors of the Longhorn.

The saloon and dance hall was crowded. A few familiar faces, but they were sullen faces, lined and hard. The faces of bitter men, defeated but not whipped. The others were new faces, the hard, tough faces of gunhands, the weather-beaten cowpunchers who had come in to take the new jobs. He pushed his way to the bar.

There were three bartenders now, and it wasn't until he ordered that the squat, fat man glanced down the bar and saw him. His jaw hardened, and he spoke to the bartender who was getting a bottle to pour Gentry's rye.

The bartender, a lean, sallow-faced man, strolled back to him. "We're not servin' you," he said. "I got my orders."

Tack reached across the bar, his hand shooting out so fast the bartender had no chance to withdraw. Catching the man by his stiff collar, two fingers inside the collar and their knuckles jammed hard into the man's Adam's apple, he jerked him to the bar.

"Pour!" he said.

The man tried to speak, but Tack gripped harder and shoved back on the knuckles. Weakly, desperately, his face turning blue, the man poured. He slopped out twice what he got in the glass, but he poured. Then Tack shoved hard, and the man brought up violently against the backbar.

Tack lifted his glass with his left hand, his eyes sweeping the crowd, all of whom had drawn back slightly. "To honest ranchers!" he said loudly and clearly, and downed his drink.

A big, hard-faced man shoved through the crowd. "Maybe you're meanin' some of us ain't honest?" he suggested.

"That's right!" Tack Gentry let his voice ring out in the room, and he heard the rattle of chips cease, and the shuffling of feet died away. The crowd was listening. "That's exactly right! There were honest men here, but they were murdered or crippled. My uncle, John Gentry, was murdered. They tried to make it look like a fair and square killin' … they stuck a gun in his hand!"

"That's right!" A man broke in. "He had a gun! I seen it!"

Tack's eyes shifted. "What hand was it in?"

"His right hand!" the man stated positively, belligerently. "I seen it!"

"Thank you, pardner," Tack said politely. "The gun was in John Gentry's right hand … and John Gentry's right hand had been paralyzed ever since Shiloh!"

"Huh?" The man who had seen the gun stepped back, his face whitening a little.

Somebody back in the crowd shouted out: "That's right! You're durn' tootin' that's right! Never could use a rope 'count of it!"

Tack looked around at the crowd, and his eyes halted on the big man. He was going to break the power of Hardin, Olney, and Soderman, and he was going to start right here.

"There's goin' to be an investigation," he said loudly, "and it'll begin down in Austin. Any of you fellers bought property from Hardin, or Olney, better get your money back."

"You're talkin' a lot!" The big man thrust toward him, his wide, heavy shoulders looking broad enough for two men. "You said some of us were thieves!"

"Thieves and murderers," Tack added. "If you're one of the worms that crawl in Hardin's tracks, that goes for you!"

The big man lunged.

"Get him, Starr!" somebody shouted loudly.

Tack Gentry suddenly felt a fierce surge of pure animal joy. He stepped back and then stepped in suddenly, and his right swung, low and hard. It caught Starr as he was coming in, caught him in the pit of the stomach. He grunted and stopped dead in his tracks, but Tack set himself and swung wickedly with both hands. His left smashed into Starr's mouth, and his right split a cut over his cheekbone. Starr staggered and fell back into the crowd. He came out of the crowd, shook his head, and charged like a bull.

Tack weaved inside of the swinging fists and impaled the bigger man on a straight, hard left hand. Then he crossed a wicked right to the cut cheek, and gore cascaded down the man's face. Tack stepped in, smashing both hands to the man's body, and then, as Starr stabbed a thumb at his eye, Tack jerked his head aside and butted Starr in the face.

His nose broken, his cheek laid open to the bone, Starr staggered back, and Tack Gentry walked in, swinging with both hands. This was the beginning. This man worked for Hardin, and he was going to be an example. When he left this room, Starr's face was going to be a sample of the crashing of Van Hardin's power. With left and right, he cut and slashed at the big man's face, and Starr, overwhelmed by the attack, helpless after that first wicked body blow, crumpled under those smashing fists. He hit the floor suddenly and lay there, moaning softly.

A man shoved through the crowd and then stopped. It was Van Hardin. He looked down at the man on the floor, then his eyes, dark with hate, lifted to meet Tack Gentry's eyes.

"Lookin' for trouble, are you?" he said.

"Only catchin' up with some that started while I was gone, Van," Tack said. He felt good. He was on the balls of his feet and ready. He had liked the jarring of blows, liked the feeling of combat. He was ready. "You should have made sure I was dead, Hardin, before you tried to steal property from a kindly old man."

"Nothing was stolen," Van Hardin said evenly, calmly. "We took only what was ours and in a strictly legal manner."

"There will be an investigation," Gentry replied bluntly, "from Austin. Then we'll thrash the whole thing out."

Hardin's eyes sharpened, and he was suddenly wary. "An investigation? What makes you think so?"

Tack was aware that Hardin was worried. "Because I'm startin' it. I'm askin' for it, and I'll get it. There was a lot you didn't know about that land you stole, Hardin. You were like most crooks. You could only see your side of the question, and it looked very simple and easy, but there's always the thing you overlook, and *you* overlooked somethin'."

The doors swung wide, and Olney pushed into the room. He stopped, glancing from Hardin to Gentry. "What goes on here?" he demanded.

"Gentry is accusin' us of bein' thieves," Hardin said carelessly.

Olney turned and faced Tack. "He's in no position to accuse anybody of anything," he said. "I'm arrestin' him for murder!"

There was a stir in the room, and Tack Gentry felt the sudden sickness of fear. "Murder? Are you crazy?" he demanded.

"I'm not, but you may he," the sheriff said. "I've just come from the office of Anson Childe. He's been murdered. You were his last visitor. You were observed sneaking into his place by the back stairs. You were observed sneaking out of it. I'm arresting you for murder."

The room was suddenly still, and Tack Gentry felt the rise of hostility toward him. Many men had admired the courage of Anson Childe; many men had been helped by him. Frightened themselves, they had enjoyed his flouting of Hardin and Olney. Now he was dead, murdered.

"Childe was my friend," Tack protested. "He was goin' to Austin for me."

Hardin laughed sarcastically. "You mean he knew you had no case and refused to go, and in a fit of rage you killed him. You shot him."

"You'll have to come with me," Olney said grimly. "You'll get a fair trial."

Silently, Tack looked at him. Swiftly, thoughts raced through his mind. There was no chance for escape. The crowd was too thick, and he had no idea if there was a horse out front, although there no doubt was, but his own horse was in the livery stable. Olney relieved him of his gun belt, and they started toward the door. Starr, leaning against the doorpost, his face raw as chewed beef, glared at him evilly.

"I'll be seein' you," he said softly. "Soon."

Soderman and Hardin had fallen in around him, and behind them were two of Hardin's roughs.

* * * * *

The jail was small, just four cells and an outer office. The door of one of the cells was opened, and he was shoved inside.

Hardin grinned at him. "This should settle the matter for Austin," he said. "Childe had friends down there."

Anson Childe murdered! Tack Gentry, numbed by the blow, stared at the stone wall. He had counted on Childe, counted on his stirring up an investigation. Once an investigation was started, he possessed two aces in the hole he could use to defeat Hardin in court, but it demanded a court not controlled by Hardin. With Childe's death he had no friends on the outside. Betty had barely spoken to him when they met, and, if she was going to work for Hardin in his dance hall, she must have changed much. Bill London was a cripple and unable to get around. Red Furness, for all his friendship, wouldn't come out in the open. Tack had no illusions about the murder. By the time the case came to trial, they would have found ample evidence. They had his guns, and they could fire two or three shots from them, whatever had been used on Childe. It would be a simple thing to frame him. Hardin would have no trouble in finding witnesses.

He was standing, staring out the small window, its lower sill just on the level of his eyes, when he heard a distant rumble of thunder and a jagged streak of lightning brightened the sky, followed by more thunder. The rains came slowly, softly, and then in steadily increasing volume. The jail was still and empty. Sounds of music and occasional shouts sounded from the Longhorn, then the roar of rain drowned them out. He threw himself down on the cot in the corner of the room and, lulled by the falling rain, was soon asleep.

* * * * *

A long time later, he awakened. The rain was still falling, but above it was another sound. Listening, he suddenly realized what it was. The dry wash behind the town was running, probably bank full. Lying there in the darkness, he became aware of still another sound, of the nearer rushing of water. Lifting his head, he listened. Then he got to his feet and crossed the small cell.

Water was running under the corner of the jail. There had been a good deal of rain lately, and he had noted that the barrel at the corner of the jail had been full. It was overflowing, and the water had evidently washed under the corner of the building.

He walked back and sat down on the bed, and, as he listened to the water, an idea came to him suddenly. Tack got up and went to the corner of the cell. Striking a match, he studied the wall and floor. Both were damp. He stamped on the stone flags of the floor, but they were solid. He kicked at the wall. It was also solid.

How thick were those walls? Judging by what he remembered of the door, the walls were all of eight inches thick, but how about the floor? Kneeling on the floor, he struck another match, studying the mortar around the corner flagstone.

Then he felt in his pockets. There was nothing there he could use to dig that mortar. His pocketknife, his bowie knife, his keys—all were gone. Suddenly, he had an inspiration. Slipping off his wide leather belt, he began to dig at the mortar with the edge of his heavy brass belt buckle.

The mortar was damp, but he worked steadily. His hands slipped on the sweaty buckle and he skinned his fingers and knuckles on the rough stone floor, yet he persevered, scraping, scratching, digging out tiny fragments of mortar. From time to time, he straightened up and stamped on the stone. It was solid as Gibraltar.

Five hours he scraped and scratched, digging until his belt buckle was no longer of use. He had scraped out almost two inches of mortar. Sweeping up the scattered grains of mortar and digging some of the mud off his boots, he filled in the cracks as best he could. Then he walked to his bunk and sprawled out and was instantly asleep.

III

Early in the morning, he heard someone stirring around outside. Then Olney walked back to his cell and looked in at him. Starr followed in a few minutes, carrying a plate of food and a pot of coffee. His face was badly bruised and swollen, and his eyes were hot with hate. He put the food down and then walked away. Olney loitered.

"Gentry," he said suddenly, "I hate to see a good hand in this spot."

Tack looked up. "I'll bet you do," he said sarcastically.

"No use takin' that attitude," Olney protested. "After all, you made trouble for us. Why couldn't you leave well enough alone? You were in the clear, you had a few dollars apparently, and you could do all right. Hardin took possession of those ranches legally. He can hold 'em, too."

"We'll see."

"No, I mean it. He can. Why don't you drop the whole thing?"

"Drop it?" Tack laughed. "How can I drop it? I'm in jail for murder now, and you know as well as I do I never killed Anson

Childe. This trial will smoke the whole story out of its hole. I mean to see that it does."

Olney winced, and Tack could see he had touched a tender spot. That was what they were afraid of. They had him now, but they didn't want him. They wanted nothing so much as to be completely rid of him.

"Only make trouble for folks," Olney protested. "You won't get nowhere. You can bet that, if you go to trial, we'll have all the evidence we need."

"Sure. I know I'll be framed."

"What can you expect?" Olney shrugged. "You're askin' for it. Why don't you play smart? If you'd leave the country, we could sort of arrange maybe to turn you loose."

Tack looked up at him. "You mean that?" *Like blazes,* he told himself. *I can see you turnin' me loose! And when I walked out, you'd have somebody there to smoke me down, shot escaping jail. Yeah, I know.* "If I thought you'd let me go ..." He hesitated, angling to get Olney's reaction.

The sheriff put his head close to the bars. "You know me, Tack," he whispered. "I don't want to see you stick your head in a noose. Sure, you spoke out of turn, and you tried to scare up trouble for us, but if you'd leave, I think I could arrange it."

"Just give me the chance," Tack assured him. "Once I get out of here, I'll really start movin'." *And that's no lie,* he added to himself.

Olney went away, and the morning dragged slowly. They would let him go. He was praying now they would wait until the next day. Yet even if they did permit him to escape, even if they did not have him shot as he was leaving, what could he do? Childe, his best means of assistance, was dead. At every turn he was stopped. They had the law, and they had the guns.

His talk the night before would have implanted doubts.

His whipping of Starr would have pleased many, and some of them would realize that his arrest for the murder of Childe was a frame. Yet none of these people would do anything about it without leadership. None of them wanted his own neck in a noose.

Olney dropped in later and leaned close to the bars. "I'll have something arranged by tomorrow," he said.

Tack lay back on the bunk and fell asleep. All day the rain had continued without interruption, except for a few minutes at a time. The hills would be soggy now, the trails bad. He could hear the wash running strongly, running like a river not thirty yards behind the jail.

Darkness fell, and he ate again and then returned to his bunk. With a good lawyer and a fair judge, he could beat them in court. He had an ace in the hole that would help and another that might do the job.

He waited until the jail was silent and he could hear the usual sounds from the Longhorn. Then he got up and walked over to the corner. All day water had been running under the corner of the jail and must have excavated a fair-size hole by now. Tack knelt down and took from his pocket the fork he had secreted after his meal.

Olney, preoccupied with plans to allow Tack Gentry to escape and sure that Tack was accepting the plan, had paid little attention to the returned plate.

On his knees, Tack dug out the loosely filled-in dust and dirt, and then began digging frantically at the hole. He worked steadily for an hour and then crossed to the bucket for a drink of water and to stretch, and then he returned to work.

Another hour passed. He got up and stamped on the stone. It seemed to sink under his feet. He bent his knees and jumped, coming down hard on his heels. The stone gave way so suddenly, he almost went through. He caught himself, withdrew his feet from the hole, and bent over, striking a match. It was no more than six inches to the surface of the water, and even a glance told him it must be much deeper than he had believed.

He took another look, waited an instant, and then lowered his feet into the water. The current jerked at them, and then he lowered his body through the hole and let go. Instantly, he was jerked away and literally thrown downstream. He caught a quick glimpse of a light from a window, and then he was whirling over and over. He grabbed frantically, hoping to get his hands on something, but they clutched only empty air. Frantically he fought toward where there must be a bank, realizing he was in a roaring stream all of six feet deep. He struck nothing and was thrown, almost hurtled, downstream with what seemed to be overwhelming speed. Something black loomed near him, and at the same instant, the water caught at him, rushing with even greater power. He grabbed again at the blob of blackness, and his hand caught a root.

Yet it was nothing secure, merely a huge cottonwood log rushing downstream. Working his way along it, he managed to get a leg over and crawled atop it. Fortunately, the log did not roll over.

Lying there in the blackness, he realized what must have happened. Behind the row of buildings that fronted on the street, of which the jail was one, was a shallow, sandy ditch. At one end of it, the bluff reared up. The dry wash skirted one side of the triangle formed by the bluff, and the ditch formed the other. Water flowing off the bluff and off the roofs of the buildings and from the street of the town and the rise beyond it had flooded into the ditch, washing it deeper. Yet now he knew he was in the current of the wash itself, now running bank full, a raging torrent.

A brief flash of lightning revealed the stream down which he was shooting like a chip in a millrace. Below, he knew, was Cathedral Gorge, a narrow, boulder-strewn gash in the mountain down which this wash would thunder like an express train. Tack had seen logs go down it, smashing into boulders, hurled against the rocky walls, and then shooting at last out into the open flat below the gorge. And he knew instantly that no living thing could hope to ride a charging log through the black, roaring depths of the gorge and come out anything but a mangled, lifeless pulp.

The log he was bestriding hit a wave, and water drenched him. Then the log whirled dizzily around a bend in the wash. Before him and around another bend, he could hear the roar of the gorge. The log swung, and then the driving roots ripped into a heap of debris at the bend of the wash, and the log swung wickedly across the current. Scrambling like a madman, Tack fought his way toward the roots, and then, even as the log ripped loose, he hurled himself at the heap of debris.

He landed in a heap of broken boughs and felt something gouge him, and then, scrambling, he made the rocks and clambered up into their shelter, lying there on a flat rock, gasping for breath.

* * * * *

A long time later, he got up. Something was wrong with his right leg. It felt numb and sore. He crawled over the rocks and stumbled over the muddy earth toward the partial shelter of a clump of trees.

He needed shelter, and he needed a gun. Tack Gentry knew that now that he was free, they would scour the country for him. They might believe him dead, but they would want to be certain. What he needed now was shelter, rest, and food. He needed to examine himself to see how badly he was injured, yet where could he turn?

Betty? She was too far away, and he had no horse. Red Furness? Possibly, but how much the man would or could help, he did not know. Yet thinking of Red made him think of Childe. There was a place for him. If he could only get to Childe's quarters over the saloon!

Luckily, he had landed on the same side of the wash as the town. He was stiff and sore, and his leg was paining him grievously. Yet there was no time to be lost. What the hour was he had no idea, but he knew his progress would be slow, and he must be careful. The rain was pounding down, but he was so wet now that it made no difference.

* * * * *

How long it took him, he never knew. He could have been no more than a mile from town, perhaps less, and he walked, crawled, and pulled himself to the edge of town and then behind the buildings, until he reached the dark back stairway to Anson Childe's room. Step by step he crawled up. Fortunately, the door was unlocked.

Once inside, he stood there in the darkness, listening. There was no sound. This room was windowless but for one very small and tightly curtained window at the top of the wall. Tack felt for the candle, found it, and fumbled for a match. When he had the candle alight, he started pulling off his clothes.

Naked, he dried himself with a towel, avoiding the injured leg. Then he found a bottle and poured himself a drink. He tossed it off, and then sat down on the edge of the bed, and looked at his leg.

It almost made him sick to look at it. Hurled against a root or something in the dark, he had torn a great, mangled wound in the calf of his leg. No artery appeared to have been injured, but in places his shinbone was visible through the ripped flesh. The wound in the calf was deeper. Cleansing it as best he could, he found a white shirt belonging to Childe and bandaged his leg.

Exhausted, he fell asleep—when, he never recalled. Only hours later he awakened suddenly to find sunlight streaming through the door into the front room. His leg was stiff and sore, and, when he moved, it throbbed with pain. Using a cane he found hanging in the room, he pulled himself up and staggered to the door.

The curtains in the front room were up, and sunlight streamed in. The rain seemed to be gone. From where he stood, he could see into the street, and almost the first person he saw was Van Hardin. He was standing in front of the Longhorn talking to Soderman and the mustached man Tack had first seen at his own ranch.

The sight reminded him, and Tack hunted around for a gun. He found a pair of beautifully matched Colts, silver-plated and ivory-handled. He strapped them on with their ornate belt and holsters. Then, standing in a corner, he found a riot gun and a Henry rifle. He checked the loads in all the guns, found several boxes of ammunition for each of them, and emptied a box of .45s into the pockets of a pair of Childe's pants he pulled on. Then he put a double handful of shotgun shells into the pockets of a leather jacket he found. He sat down then, for he was weak and trembling.

IV

His time was short. Sooner or later someone would come to this room. Either someone would think of it or someone would come to claim the room for himself. Red Furness had no idea he was there, so would probably not hesitate to let anyone come up.

He locked the door and then dug around and found a stale loaf of bread and some cheese. Then he lay down to rest. His leg was throbbing with pain, and he knew it needed care, and badly.

When he awakened, he studied the street from a vantage point well inside the room and to one side of the window. Several knots of men were standing around talking, more men than should have been in town at that hour. He recognized one or two of them as being old-timers. Twice he saw Olney ride by, and the sheriff was carrying a riot gun.

Starr and the mustached man were loafing in front of the Longhorn, and two other men Tack recognized as coming from the old London Ranch were there.

He ate some more bread and cheese. He was just finishing his sandwich when a buckboard turned into the street, and his heart jumped when he saw Betty London was driving. Beside her in the seat was her father, Bill, worn and old, his hair white now, but he was wearing a gun!

Something was stirring down below. It began to look as if the lid was about to blow off. Yet Tack had no idea of his own status. He was an escaped prisoner and as such could be shot on sight legally by Olney or Starr, who seemed to be a deputy. From the wary attitude of the Van Hardin men, he knew that they were disturbed by their lack of knowledge of him.

Yet the day passed without incident, and finally he returned to the bunk and lay down after checking his guns once more. The time for the payoff was near, he knew. It could come at any moment. He was lying there, thinking about that and looking up at the rough plank ceiling, when he heard steps on the stairs.

He arose so suddenly that a twinge of pain shot through the weight that had become his leg. The steps were on the front stairs, not the back. A quick glance from the window told him it was Betty London. What did she want here?

Her hand fell on the knob, and it turned. He eased off the bed and turned the key in the lock. She hesitated just an instant, and then stepped in. When their eyes met, hers went wide, and her face went white to the lips.

"You!" she gasped. "Oh, Tack! What have you been doing? Where have you been?"

She started toward him, but he backed up and sat down on the bed.

"Wait. Do they know I'm up here?" he demanded harshly.

"No, Tack. I came up to see if some papers were here, some papers I gave to Anson Childe before he was … murdered."

"You think I did that?" he demanded.

"No, of course not." Her eyes held a question. "Tack, what's the matter? Don't you like me anymore?"

"Don't I like you?" His lips twisted with bitterness. "Lady, you've got a nerve to ask that. I come back and find my girl about to go dancin' in a cheap saloon dance hall, and …"

"I needed money, Tack," Betty said quietly. "Dad needed care. We didn't have any money. Everything we had was lost when we lost the ranch. Hardin offered me the job. He said he wouldn't let anybody molest me."

"What about him?"

"I could take care of him." She looked at him, puzzled. "Tack, what's the matter? Why are you sitting down? Are you hurt?"

"My leg." He shook his head as she started forward. "Don't bother about it. There's no time. What are they saying down there? What's all the crowd in town? Give it to me, quick."

"Some of them think you were drowned in escaping from jail. I don't think Van Hardin thinks that, nor Olney. They seem very disturbed. The crowd is in town for Childe's funeral and because some of them think you were murdered once Olney got you in jail. Some of our old friends."

"Betty!" The call came from the street below. It was Van Hardin's voice.

"Don't answer." Tack Gentry got up. His dark green eyes were hard. "I want him to come up."

Betty waited, her eyes wide, listening. Footsteps sounded on the stairway, and then the door shoved open. "Bet—" Van Hardin's voice died out, and he stood there, one hand on the doorknob, staring at Tack.

"Howdy, Hardin," Tack said, "I was hopin' you'd come."

Van Hardin said nothing. His powerful shoulders filled the open door, his eyes were set, and the shock was fading from them now.

"Got a few things to tell you, Hardin," Tack continued gently. "Before you go out of this feet first, I want you to know what a sucker you've been."

"A sucker I've been?" Hardin laughed. "What chance have you got? The street down there is full of my men. You've friends there, too, but they lack leadership. They don't know what to do. My men have their orders. And then I won't have any trouble with you, Gentry. Your old friends around here told me all about you. Soft, like that uncle of yours."

"Ever hear of Black Jack Paris, Hardin?"

"The gunman? Of course, but what's he got to do with you?"

"Nothin', now. He did once ... up in Ellsworth, Kansas. They dug a bed for him next mornin', Hardin. He was too slow. You said I was soft? Well, maybe I was once. Maybe in spots I still am, but you see, since the folks around here have seen me, I've been over the cattle trails, been doin' some Injun fightin' and rustler killin'. It makes a sight of change in a man, Hardin. But that ain't what I wanted you to know. I wanted you to know what a fool you were, tryin' to steal our ranch. You see, the land in our home ranch wasn't like the rest of this land, Hardin."

"What do you mean?" Hardin demanded suspiciously.

"Why, you're the smart boy," Tack drawled easily. "You should have checked before takin' so much for granted. You see, the Gentry Ranch was a land grant. My grandmother, she was a Basque, see? The land came to us through her family, and the will she left was that it would belong to us as long as any of us lived, that it couldn't be sold or traded, and in case we all died, it was to go to the state of Texas."

Van Hardin stared. "What?" he gasped. "What kind of fool deal is this you're givin' me?"

"Fool deal is right," Tack said quietly. "You see, the state of Texas knows no Gentry would sell or trade, knowin' we couldn't, so if somebody else showed up with the land, they were bound to ask a sight of questions. Sooner or later they'd have got around to askin' you how come."

Hardin seemed stunned. From the street below, there was a sound of horses' hoofs.

Then a voice said from Tack's left: "You better get out, Van. There's talkin' to be done in the street. I want Tack Gentry."

Tack's head jerked around. It was Soderman. The short, squinty-eyed man was staring at him, gun in hand. He heard Hardin turn and bolt out of the room, saw resolution in Soderman's eyes. Hurling himself toward the wall, Gentry's hand flashed for his pistol.

A gun blasted in the room with a roar like a cannon, and Gentry felt the angry whip of the bullet, and then he fired twice, low down. Soderman fell back against the doorjamb, both hands grabbing at his stomach, just below his belt buckle.

"You shot me!" he gasped, round-eyed. "You shot … me!"

"Like you did my uncle," Tack said coolly. "Only you had better than an even break, and he had no break at all."

Gentry could feel blood from the opened wound trickling down his leg. He glanced at Betty. "I've got to get down there," he said. "He's a slick talker."

Van Hardin was standing down in the street. Beside him was Olney, and nearby was Starr. Other men, a half dozen of them, loitered nearby.

Slowly, Tack Gentry began stumping down the stair. All eyes looked up. Red Furness saw him and spoke out: "Tack, these three men are Rangers come down from Austin to make some inquiries."

Hardin pointed at Gentry. "He's wanted for murdering Anson Childe! Also for jailbreaking, and, unless I'm much mistaken, he has killed another man up there in Childe's office!"

The Rangers looked at him curiously, and then one of them glanced at Hardin. "You-all the hombre what lays claim to the Gentry place?"

Hardin swallowed quickly, and then his eyes shifted. "No, that was Soderman. The man who was upstairs." Hardin looked at Tack Gentry. With the Rangers here, he knew his game was played out. He smiled suddenly. "You've nothin' on me at all, gents," he said coolly. "Soderman killed John Gentry and laid claim to his ranch. I don't know nothin' about it."

"You engineered it!" Bill London burst out. "Same as you did the stealin' of my ranch!"

"You've no proof," Hardin sneered. "Not a particle. My name is on no papers, and you have no evidence."

Coolly, he strode across to his black horse and swung into the saddle. He was smiling gently, but there was sneering triumph behind the smile. "You've nothin' on me, not a thing."

"Don't let him get away!" Bill London shouted. "He's the worst one of the whole kit and kaboodle of 'em!"

"But he's right," the Ranger protested. "In all the papers we've found, there's not a single item to tie him up. If he's in it, he's been almighty smart."

"Then arrest him for horse stealin'," Tack Gentry said. "That's my black horse he's on."

Hardin's face went cold, and then he smiled. "Why, that's crazy! That's foolish," he said. "This is my horse. I reared him from a colt. Anybody could be mistaken, 'cause one black horse is like another. My brand's on him, and you can all see it's an old brand."

Tack Gentry stepped out in front of the black horse. "Button!" he said sharply. "Button!"

At the familiar voice, the black horse's head jerked up.

"Button!" Tack called. "Hut! Hut!"

As the name and the sharp command rolled out, Button reacted like an explosion of dynamite. He jumped straight up in the air and came down hard. Then he sunfished wildly, and Van Hardin hit the dirt in a heap.

"Button!" Tack commanded. "Go get Blackie!"

Instantly, the horse wheeled and trotted to the hitching rail where Blackie stood ground-hitched as Olney had left him. Button caught the reins in his teeth and led the other black horse back.

The Ranger grinned. "Reckon, mister," he said, "you done proved your case. The man's a horse thief."

Hardin climbed to his feet, his face dark with fury. "You think you'll get away with that?" His hand flashed for his gun.

Tack Gentry had been watching him, and now his own hand moved down and then up. The two guns barked as one. A chip flew from the stair post beside Tack, but Van Hardin turned slowly and went to his knees in the dust.

At almost the same instant, a sharp voice rang out: "Olney! Starr!"

Olney's face went white, and he wheeled, hand flashing for his gun. "Anson Childe," he gasped.

Childe stood on the platform in front of his room and fired once, twice, three times. Sheriff Olney went down, coughing and muttering. Starr backed through the swinging doors of the saloon and sat down hard in the sawdust.

Tack stared at him. "What the …?"

The tall young lawyer came down the steps. "Fooled them, didn't I? They tried to get me once too often. I got their man with a shotgun in the face. Then I changed clothes with him and lit out for Austin. I came in with the Rangers, and then left them on the edge of town. They told me they'd let us have it our way unless they were needed."

"Saves the state of Texas a sight of money," one of the Rangers drawled. "Anyway, we been checkin' on this here Hardin. On Olney, too. That's why they wanted to keep things quiet around here. They knowed we was checkin' on 'em."

The Rangers moved in and, with the help of a few of the townspeople, rounded up Hardin's other followers.

Tack grinned at the lawyer. "Lived up to your name, pardner," he said. "You sure did! All your sheep in the fold, now."

"What do you mean? Lived up to my name?" Anson Childe looked around.

Gentry grinned. "'And a little Childe shall lead them,'" he said.

MCQUEEN OF THE TUMBLING K

Ward McQueen reined in the strawberry roan and squinted his eyes against the sun. Salty sweat made his eyes smart, and he dabbed at them with the end of a bandanna. Kim Sartain was hazing a couple of rambunctious steers back into line. Bud Fox was walking his horse up the slope to where Ward waited, watching the drive.

Fox drew up alongside him and said: "Ward, d'you remember that old brindle ladino with the scarred hide? This here is his range, but we haven't seen hide nor hair of him."

"That's one old mossyhorn I won't forget in a hurry. He's probably hiding back in one of the canyons. Have you cleaned them out yet?"

"Uhn-huh, we surely have. Baldy an' me both worked 'em, and no sign of him. Makes a body mighty curious."

"Yeah, I suppose you've got a point. It ain't like him to be away from the action. He'd surely be down there makin' trouble." He paused, suddenly thoughtful. "Missed any other stock since I've been gone?"

Fox shrugged. "If there's any missin', it can't be more than a few head, but you can bet if that old crowbait is gone, some others went with him. He ramrods a good-sized herd all by himself."

Baldy Jackson joined them on the slope. He jerked his head to indicate a nearby canyon mouth. "Seen some mighty queer tracks over yonder," he said, "like a man afoot."

"We'll go have a look," McQueen said. "A man afoot in this country? It isn't likely."

He started the roan across the narrow valley, with Baldy and Bud following.

The canyon was narrow and high-walled. Parts of it were choked with brush and fallen rock, with only the winding watercourse to offer a trail. In the spreading fan of sand where the wash emptied into the valley, Baldy drew up.

Ward looked down at the tracks Baldy indicated. "Yes, they do look odd," said Ward. "Fixed him some homemade footgear. Wonder if that's his blood or some critter?" Leading the roan, he followed the tracks up the dry streambed.

After a few minutes, he halted. "He's been hurt. Look at the tracks headed this way. Fairly long, steady stride. I'd guess he's a tall man. But see here? Goin' back, the steps are shorter an' he's staggerin'. He stopped twice in twenty yards, each time to lean against something."

"Reckon we'd better follow him?" Baldy looked at the jumble of boulders and crowded brush. "If he doesn't aim to be ketched, he could make us a powerful lot of trouble."

"We'll follow him anyway. Baldy, you go back an' help the boys. Tell Kim an' Tennessee where we're at. Bud will stay with me. Maybe we can track him down, an' he should be grateful. It looks like he's hurt bad."

They moved along cautiously for another hundred yards. Bud Fox stopped, mopping his face. "He doesn't figure on bein' followed. He's makin' a try at losin' his trail. Even tried to wipe out a spot of blood."

Ward McQueen paused and looked up the watercourse with keen, probing eyes. There was something wrong about all this. He had been riding this range for months now and believed he knew it well, yet he remembered no such man as this must be and had seen no such tracks. Obviously, the man was injured. Just as obviously he was trying, even in his weakened condition, to obliterate his trail. That meant that he expected to be followed and that those who followed were enemies.

Pausing to study the terrain, he ran over in his mind the possibilities from among those who he knew. Who might the injured man be? And who did he fear?

They moved on, working out the trail in the close, hot air of the canyon. The tracks split suddenly and disappeared on a wide ledge of stone where the canyon divided into two.

"We're stuck," Fox said. "He won't leave tracks with those makeshift shoes of his, and there's nowhere he can go up the canyons."

The right-hand branch ended in a steep, rocky slide, impossible to climb without hours of struggle, and the left branch ended against the sheer face of a cliff against whose base lay a heaped-up pile of boulders and rocky debris.

"He may have doubled back or hidden in the brush," Fox added.

Ward shrugged. "Let's go back. He doesn't want to be found, but hurt like he is, he's apt to die out here without care."

Deliberately, he had spoken loudly. Turning their mounts, they rode back down the canyon to rejoin the herd.

* * * * *

Ruth Kermitt was waiting on the steps when they left the grassy bottom and rode up to the bunkhouse. With her was a slender, narrow-faced man in a black frock coat. As Ward drew up, the man's all-encompassing glance took him in, then slid away.

"Ward, this is Jim Yount. He's buying cattle and wants to look at the herd you just brought in."

"Howdy," Ward said agreeably. He glanced at Yount's horse and then at the tied-down gun.

Two more men sat on the steps of the bunkhouse. A big man in a checkered shirt and a slim redhead with a rifle across his knees.

"We're looking to buy five hundred to a thousand head," Yount commented. "We heard you had good stock."

"Beef?"

"No, breeding stock, mostly. We're stockin' a ranch. I'm locatin' the other side of Newton's place."

Ward commented: "We have some cattle. Or rather, Miss Kermitt has. I'm just the foreman."

"Oh?" Yount looked around at Ruth with a quick, flashing smile. "Miss, is it? Or are you a widow?"

"Miss. My brother and I came here together, but he was killed."

"Hard for a young woman to run a ranch alone, isn't it?" His smile was sympathetic.

"Miss Kermitt does very well," Ward replied coolly, "and she isn't exactly alone."

"Oh?" Yount glanced at McQueen, one eyebrow lifted. "No," he said after a minute, "I don't expect you could say she was alone as long as she had cattle on the place, and cowhands."

Ruth got up quickly, not liking the look on Ward's face. "Mr. Yount? Wouldn't you like some coffee? Then we can talk business."

When they had gone inside, Ward McQueen turned on his heel and walked to the bunkhouse, leading his horse. He was mad, and he didn't care who knew it. The thin-faced redhead looked at him as he drew near.

"What's the matter, friend? Somebody steal your girl?"

Ward McQueen halted and turned slowly. Baldy Jackson got up quickly and moved out of line. The move put him at the corner of the bunkhouse, leaving Yount's riders at the apex of a triangle of which McQueen and himself formed the two corners.

"Miss Kermitt," McQueen's tone was cold, "is my boss. She is also a lady. Don't get any funny notions."

The redhead chuckled. "Yeah, and our boss is a ladies' man. He knows how to handle 'em." Deliberately, he turned his back on Baldy. "Never been foreman on a place like this, Dodson. Maybe you or me will have a new job."

Ward walked into the bunkhouse. Bud Fox was loitering beside the window. He, too, had been watching the pair.

"Don't seem the friendly type," Bud commented, pouring warm water into the tin washbasin. "Almost like they wanted trouble."

"What would be the idea of that?" Ward inquired.

Bud was splashing in the basin and made no reply, but Ward wondered. Certainly their attitude was not typical. He glanced toward the house, and his lips tightened. Jim Yount was a slick-talking sort and probably a woman would think him good-looking.

Out beyond the ranch house was a distant light, which would be Gelvin's store in Mannerhouse. Gelvin had ranched the country beyond Newton's. Suddenly, McQueen made up his mind. After chow he would ride into Mannerhouse and have a little talk with Gelvin.

Supper was served in the ranch house, as always, and was a

quiet meal but for Ruth and Jim Yount, who laughed and talked at the head of the table.

Ward, seated opposite Yount, had little to say. Baldy, Bud, and Tennessee sat in strict silence. Only Red Lund, seated beside Pete Dodson, occasionally ventured a remark. At the foot of the table, lean, wiry Kim Sartain let his eyes rove from face to face.

When supper was over, Ward moved outside into the moonlight, and Kim followed.

"What goes on?" Kim whispered. "I never did see anybody so quiet."

Ward explained, adding: "Yount may be a cattle buyer, but the two riders with him are no average cowpunchers. Red Lund is a gunhand if I ever saw one, and Dodson's right off the Owlhoot Trail or I miss my guess." He hitched his belt. "I'm ridin' into town. Keep an eye on things, will you?"

"I'll do that." He lowered his tone. "That Lund now? I don't cotton to him. Nor Yount," he added.

* * * * *

Gelvin's store was closed, but McQueen knew where to find him. Swinging down from the saddle, he tied his horse and pushed through the batwing doors. Abel was polishing glasses behind the bar, and Gelvin was at a table with Dave Cormack, Logan Keane, and a tall, lean-bodied stranger. They were playing poker.

Two other strangers lounged at the bar. They turned to look at him as he came in.

"Howdy, Ward! How's things at the Tumblin' K?"

The two men at the bar turned abruptly and looked at Ward again—quick, searching glances. He had started to speak to Gelvin, but something warned him and instead he walked to the bar.

"Pretty good," he replied. "Diggin' some stuff out of the brakes today. Tough work. All right for a brush-popper, but I like open country."

He tossed off his drink, watching the two men in the bar mirror. "They tell me there's good range beyond Newton's. I think I'll ride over and see if there's any lyin' around loose."

Gelvin glanced up. He was a short, rather handsome man with a keen, intelligent face.

"There's plenty that you can have for the taking. That country is going back to desert as fast as it can. Sand moving in, streams drying up. You can ride a hundred miles and never find a drink. Why ..." He picked up the cards and began to shuffle them. "Old Coyote Benny Chait came in two or three weeks ago. He was heading out of the country. He got euchred out of his ranch by some slick card handler. He was laughin' at the man who won it, said he'd get enough of the country in a hurry."

The two men at the bar had turned and were listening to Gelvin. One of them started to speak, and the other put a cautioning hand on his arm.

"Who was it won the ranch? Did he say?"

"Sure." Gelvin began to deal. "Some driftin' cardsharp by the name of ..."

"You talk too much!" The larger of the two men at the bar stepped toward the card table. "What d'you know about the country beyond Newton's?"

Startled by the unprovoked attack, Gelvin turned in his chair. His eyes went from one to the other of the two men. Ward McQueen had picked up the bottle.

"What is this?" Gelvin asked, keeping his tone even. These men did not seem to be drunk, yet he was experienced enough to know he was in trouble, serious trouble. "What did I say? I was just commenting on the country beyond Newton's."

"You lied!" The big man's hand was near his gun. "You lied! That country ain't goin' back! It's as good as it ever was!"

Gelvin was a stubborn man. This man was trying to provoke a fight, but Gelvin had no intention of being killed over a trifle. "I did not lie," he replied coolly. "I lived in that country for ten years. I came in with the first white men, and I've talked with the Indians who were there earlier. I know of what I speak."

"Then you're sayin' I'm a liar?" The big man's hand spread over his gun.

Ward McQueen turned in one swift movement. His right hand knocked the bottle spinning toward the second man, and he kept swinging around, his right hand grabbing the big man by the belt. With a heave he swung the big man off balance and whirled him, staggering, into the smaller man who had sprung back to avoid the bottle.

The big man staggered again, fell, and then came up with a grunt of fury. Reaching his feet, his hand went to his gun, then froze. He was looking into a gun in Ward McQueen's hand.

"That was a private conversation," Ward said mildly. "In this town we don't interfere. Understand?"

"If you didn't have the drop on me, you wouldn't be talkin' so big!"

Ward dropped his six-gun into its holster. "All right, now you've got an even break."

The two men faced him, and suddenly neither liked what they saw. This was no time for bravery, they decided.

"We ain't lookin' for trouble," the smaller man said. "We just rode into town for a drink."

"Then ride out," Ward replied. "And don't butt into conversations that don't concern you."

"Hollier an' me . . ." the big man started to speak, but then suddenly stopped and started for the door.

Ward stepped back toward the bar. "Thanks, Gelvin. You told me something I needed to know."

"I don't get it," Gelvin protested. "What made them mad?"

"That card shark you mentioned? His name wouldn't be Jim Yount, would it?"

"Of course! How did you know?"

The tall stranger playing cards with Gelvin glanced up and their eyes met. "You wouldn't be the Ward McQueen from down Texas way, would you?"

"That's where I'm from. Why?"

The man smiled pleasantly. "You cut a wide swath down thataway. I heard about your run-in with the Maravillas Canyon outfit."

* * * * *

McQueen was cautious when he took the trail to the Tumbling K, but he saw nothing of the two men in the saloon. Hollier—he was the smaller one. There had been a Hollier who escaped from a lynch mob down Uvalde way a few years back. He had trailed around with a man called Packer, and the larger of these two men had a P burned on his holster with a branding iron.

What was Jim Yount's game? Obviously, the two men from the saloon were connected with him somehow. They had seemed anxious Yount's name not be spoken, and they seemed eager to quiet any talk about the range beyond Newton's.

The available facts were few. Yount had won a ranch in a poker game. Gelvin implied the game was crooked. The ranch he won was going back to desert. In other words, he had won nothing but trouble. What came next?

The logical thing for a man of Yount's stamp was to shrug off the whole affair and go on about his business. He was not doing that, which implied some sort of a plan. Lund and Dodson would make likely companions to Packer and Hollier. Yount was talking of buying cattle, but he was not the sort to throw good money after bad. Did they plan to rustle the cattle?

One thing was sure: it was time he got back to the ranch to alert the boys for trouble. It would be coming sooner, perhaps, because of what happened tonight. But what about Ruth? Was she taken with Yount? Or simply talking business and being polite? Did he dare express his doubts to her?

The Tumbling K foreman was riding into the ranch yard when the shot rang out. Something had struck a wicked blow on his head, and he was already falling when he heard the shot.

* * * * *

His head felt constricted, as if a tight band had been drawn around his temples. Slowly, fighting every inch of the way, he battled his way to consciousness. His lids fluttered, then closed, too weak to force themselves open. He struggled against the heaviness and finally got his eyes open. He was lying on his back in a vague half-light. The air felt damp, cool.

Awareness came. He was in a cave or mine tunnel. Turning his head carefully, he looked around. He was lying on a crude pallet on a sandy floor. Some twenty feet away was a narrow shaft of light. Nearby his gun belt hung on a peg driven into the wall, and his rifle leaned against the wall.

The rift of light was blotted out, and someone crawled into the cave. A man came up and threw down an armful of wood. Then he lighted a lantern and glanced at McQueen.

"Come out of it, did you? Man, I thought you never would."

He was lean and old, with twinkling blue eyes and almost

white hair. He was long and tall. Ward noted the footgear suddenly. This was the man they had trailed up the canyon!

"Who are you?" he demanded.

The man smiled and squatted on his heels. "Charlie Quayle's the name. Used to ride for Chait, over beyond Newton's."

"You're the one we trailed up the canyon the other day. Yesterday, I believe it was."

"I'm the man, all right, but it wasn't yesterday. You've been lyin' here all of two weeks, delirious most of the time. I was beginning to believe you'd never come out of it."

"Two weeks?" McQueen struggled to sit up, but the effort was too much. He sank back. "Two weeks? They'll figure I'm dead back at the ranch. Why did you bring me here? Who shot me?"

"Hold your horses. I've got to wash up and fix some grub." He poured water in a basin and began to wash his face and hands. As he dried his hands, he explained. "You was shot, and I ain't sure who done it. Two of them rustlin' hands of Yount's packed you to the canyon and dropped you into the wash. Then they caved sand over you and some brush. But they weren't about to do more than need be, so figurin' you were sure enough dead, they rode off. I was almighty curious to know who'd been killed, so I pulled the brush away and dug into the pile and found you was still alive. I packed you up here, and, mister, it took some packin'. You're a mighty heavy man."

"Were you trailin' them when they shot me?"

"No. To tell you the truth, I was scoutin' the layout at the ranch, figurin' to steal some coffee when I heard the shot. Then I saw them carry you off, so I follered." Quayle lighted his pipe. "There's been some changes," he added. "You friend Sartain has been fired. So have Fox and that bald-headed gent. Tennessee had a run-in with Lund, and Lund killed him. Picked a fight and then beat him to the draw. Yount is real friendly with Ruth Kermitt, and he's runnin' the ranch. One or more of those tough gunmen of his is there all the time."

Ward lay back on his pallet. Kim Sartain fired! It didn't seem reasonable. Kim had been with Ruth Kermitt longer than any of them. He had been with them when Ruth and her brother came over the trail from Montana. Kim had been with her through all that trouble at Pilot Range when Ward himself had first joined them. Kim had always ridden for the brand. Now he had been fired, run off the place. And Tennessee killed!

What sort of girl was Ruth Kermitt? She had fired her oldest and most loyal hands and taken on a bunch of rustlers with a tinhorn gambler for a boss. And to think he had been getting soft on her! He'd actually been thinking she was the girl for him, and the only reason he'd held off was because he had no money, nothing to offer a woman. Well, this showed what a fool he would have been.

"You've got a hard head," Quayle was saying, "or you'd be dead by now. That bullet hit right over your eye and skidded around your skull under the skin. Laid your scalp open. You had a concussion, too. I know the signs. And you lost blood."

"I've got to get out of here," Ward said. "I've got to see Ruth Kermitt."

"You'd be better off to sit tight and get well. Right now she's right busy with that there Yount. Rides all over the range with him, holdin' hands more'n half the time. Everybody's seen 'em. And if she fired all the rest of her hands, you can be sure she doesn't want her foreman back."

He was right, of course. What good would it do even to talk to a woman who would fire such loyal hands as she'd had?

"Where d'you fit into all this?"

Quayle sliced bacon into a frying pan. "Like I told you.

I rode for Chait. Yount rooked him out of his ranch, but as a matter of fact, Chait was glad to get shut of it. When Yount found what he'd won, he was sore. Me, I'd saved me nigh on a year's wages an' was fixin' to set up for myself. One of those hands of Yount's, he seen the money and trailed me down, said it was ranch money. We had us a fight and they got some lead into me. I got away an' holed up in this here canyon."

* * * * *

All day McQueen rested in the cave, his mind busy with the problem. But what could he do? If Ruth Kermitt had made her choice, it was no longer any business of his. The best thing he could do was to get his horse and ride out of there, just drop the whole thing.

It was well after dark before Quayle returned, but he had news and was eager to talk.

"That Yount is takin' over the country! He went into Mannerhouse last night, huntin' Gelvin, but Gelvin had gone off with that stranger friend of his that he plays poker with all the time. Yount had words with Dave Cormack and killed him. They say this Yount is greased lightning with a gun. Then Lund an' Pete Dodson pistol-whipped Logan Keane. Yount told them he was runnin' the Tumblin' K and was going to marry Ruth Kermitt, and he was fed up with the talk about him and his men. He thinks he's got that town treed, an' maybe he has. Takes some folks a long time to get riled."

Ruth to marry Jim Yount! Ward felt a sharp pang. He realized suddenly that he was in love with Ruth. Now that he realized it, he knew he had been in love with her for a long time. And she was to marry Yount.

"Did you see anything of Kim Sartain?"

"No," Quayle replied, "but I heard the three of them rode over into the range beyond Newton's."

* * * * *

Ward McQueen was up at daybreak. He rolled out of his blankets, and although his head ached, he felt better. No matter. It was time to be up and doing. His long period of illness had at least given him rest, and his strength was such that he recovered rapidly. He oiled his guns and reloaded them. Quayle watched him preparing to travel but said nothing until he pulled on his boots. "Better wait until sundown if you're huntin' trouble," he said. "I got a hoss for you. Stashed him down in the brush."

"A horse? Good for you! I'm going to have a look at the ranch. This deal doesn't figure right to me."

"Nor me." Quayle knocked the ash from his pipe. "I seen that girl's face today. They rid past as I lay in the brush. She surely didn't look like a happy woman. Not like she was ridin' with a man she loved. Maybe she ain't willin'."

"I don't like to think she'd take up with a man like Yount. Well, tonight I ride."

"We ride," Quayle insisted. "I didn't like gettin' shot up any more than you-all. I'm in this fight, too."

"I can use the help, but what I'd really like you to do is hunt down Kim Sartain and the others. I can use their help. Get them back here for a showdown. Warn them it won't be pretty."

Where Quayle had found the quick-stepping buckskin, Ward neither knew nor cared. He needed a horse desperately, and the buckskin was not only a horse but a very good one.

Whatever Yount's game was, he had been fast and thorough. He had moved in on the Tumbling K, had Ward McQueen dry-gulched, had Ruth Kermitt fire her old hands, replaced them with his own men, and then rode into Mannerhouse and quieted all outward opposition by killing Dave Cormack and beating another man. If there was to have been opposition, it would have been Cormack and Keane who would have led it. Tennessee, too, had been killed, but Tennessee was not known in town, and that might be passed off as a simple dispute between cowhands. Yount had proved to be fast, ruthless, and quick of decision. As he acted with the real or apparent consent of Ruth Kermitt, there was nothing to be done by the townspeople in the village of Mannerhouse.

Probably, with Cormack and Keane out of the picture and Gelvin off God knew where, they were not inclined to do anything. None of them was suffering any personal loss, and nothing was to be gained by bucking a man already proven to be dangerous. Obviously, the gambler was in control. He had erred in only two things: he had failed to kill Charlie Quayle and to make sure that McQueen was dead.

The buckskin had a liking for the trail and moved out fast. Ward rode toward the Tumbling K, keeping out of sight. Quayle had ridden off earlier in the day to find Kim Sartain, Baldy Jackson, and Bud Fox. The latter two were good cowhands and trustworthy, but the slim, dark-faced youngster, Kim Sartain, was one of the fastest men with a gun Ward had ever seen.

"With him," Ward told the buckskin, "I'd tackle an army."

He left the buckskin in a clump of willows near the stream and then crossed on stepping-stones, working his way through the brush toward the Tumbling K ranch house.

He had no plan of action or anything on which to base a plan. If he could find Ruth and talk to her, or if he could figure out what it was that Yount was trying to accomplish, it would be a beginning.

The windows were brightly lit. For a time he lay in the

brush, studying the situation. An error now would be fatal, if not to him, at least to their plans.

There would be someone around, he was sure. Quayle had said one of the gunmen was always on the ranch, for the gambler was a careful man.

A cigarette glowed suddenly from the steps of the bunkhouse. Evidently, the man had just turned toward him. Had he inadvertently made a sound? At least he knew that somebody was there, on guard.

Ward eased off to the left until the house was between himself and the guard. Then he crossed swiftly to the side of the house. He eased a window a little higher. It was a warm night, and the window had been open at the bottom.

Jim Yount was playing solitaire at the dining room table. Red Lund was oiling a pistol. Packer was leaning his elbows on the table and smoking, watching Yount's cards.

"I always wanted a ranch," Yount was saying, "and this is it. No use gallivanting around the country when a man can live in style. I'd have had it over beyond Newton's if that damned sand bed I got from Chait had been any good. Then I saw this place. It was too good to be true."

"You worked fast," Packer said, "but you had a streak of luck when Hollier an' me got McQueen. From what I hear, he was nobody to fool around with."

Yount shrugged. "Maybe so, but all sorts of stories get started, and half of them aren't true. He might be fast with a gun, but he had no brains, and it takes brains to win in this kind of game." He glanced at Lund. "Look, that Logan Keane outfit lies south of Horsetail Creek, and it joins onto this one. Nice piece of country, thousands of acres with good water, running right up to the edge of town. Keane's scared now. Once me and Ruth Kermitt are married so our title to this ranch is cinched, we'll go to work on Keane. We'll rustle his stock, run off his hands, and force him to sell. I figure the whole job shouldn't take more than a month, at the outside."

Red glanced up from his pistol. "You get the ranches, what do we get?"

Yount smiled. "You don't want a ranch, and I do, but I happen to know that Ruth has ten thousand dollars cached. You boys ..." For a moment his eyes held those of Red Lund. "... Can split that among you. You can work out some way of dividing it even up all around."

Lund's eyes showed his understanding, and McQueen glanced at Packer, but the big horse thief showed no sign of having seen the exchange of glances. Ward could see how the split would be made; it would be done with Red Lund's six-shooter. They would get the lead; he'd take the cash. It had the added advantage to Jim Yount of leaving only one witness to his treachery.

Crouched below the window, Ward McQueen calculated his chances. Jim Yount was reputed to be a fast man with a gun. Red Lund had already proved his skill. Packer would also be good, even if not an artist like the others. Three to one made the odds much too long, and at the bunkhouse would be Hollier and Pete Dodson, neither a man to be trifled with.

A clatter of horses' hoofs on the hard-packed trail, and a horseman showed briefly in the door and was ushered into the room. It was the lean stranger who had played poker with Gelvin and Keane.

"You Jim Yount? Just riding by and wanted to tell you there's an express package at the station for Miss Kermitt. She can drop in tomorrow to pick it up, if she likes."

"Express package? Why didn't you bring it out?"

"Wouldn't let me. Seems like its money or something like

that. A package of dinero that's payment for some property in Wyoming. She's got to sign for it herself. They won't let anybody else have it."

Yount nodded. "All right. She's asleep, I think, but come morning I'll tell her."

The rider went out, and a few minutes later, Ward heard his horse's hoofs on the trail.

"More money?" Packer grinned. "Not bad, boss! She can pick it up for us, and we'll split it."

Red Lund was wiping off his pistol. "I don't like it," he spoke suddenly. "Looks like a move to get us off the ranch and the girl into town."

Yount shrugged. "I doubt it, but suppose that's it? Who in town has the guts or the skill to tackle us? Personally I believe it's the truth, but if it ain't, why worry? We'll send Packer in ahead to scout. If there's any strangers around, he can warn us. I think it's all right. We'll ride in tomorrow."

* * * * *

An hour later, and far back on a brush-covered hillside, Ward McQueen bedded down for the night. From where he lay, he could see anybody who arrived at or left the ranch. One thing he knew: tomorrow was the payoff. Ruth Kermitt would not be returning to the ranch.

At daylight he was awake and watching, his buckskin saddled and ready. It had been a damp, uncomfortable night, and he stretched, trying to get the chill from his muscles. The sunshine caught reflected light from the window. Hollier emerged and began roping horses in the corral. He saddled his own, Ruth's brown mare, and Yount's big gray.

Ward McQueen tried to foresee what would happen. He was

convinced, as was Red Lund, that the package was a trick. There were only nine buildings on the town's main street, scarcely more than two dozen houses scattered about. The express and stage office was next to the saloon. Gelvin's store was across the street.

Whatever happened, Ruth would be in danger. She would be with Yount, closely surrounded by the others. To fire on them was to endanger her.

And where did that young rider stand? He had been called Rip, and he had known of McQueen's gun battle in Maravillas Canyon. Ward was sure he was not the aimless drifter he was supposed to be. His face was too keen, his eyes too sharp. If he had baited a trap with money, he had used the only bait to which these men would rise. But what was he hoping to accomplish?

There were no men in Mannerhouse who could draw a gun in the same league with Yount or Lund. Gelvin would try, if he was there, but Gelvin had only courage and no particular skill with a handgun, and courage alone was not enough.

It was an hour after daylight when Packer mounted his paint gelding and started for town. Ward watched him go, speculating on what must follow. He had resolved upon his own course of action. His was no elaborate plan. He intended to slip into town and, at the right moment, kill Jim Yount and, if possible, Red Lund.

The only law in Mannerhouse was old John Binns, a thoroughly good man of some seventy years who had been given the job largely in lieu of a pension. He had been a hard-working man who owned his home and a few acres of ground, and he had a wife only a few years younger.

Mannerhouse had never been on the route of trail drives, land booms, or mining discoveries, and in consequence the town had few disturbances or characters likely to cause them. The jail had been used but once, when the town first came into being, and few citizens could remember the occasion. John Binns's enforcement of the law usually was a quiet suggestion to be a little less noisy or to go home and sleep it off.

Ward McQueen, a law-abiding man, found himself faced with a situation where right, justice, and the simple rules of civilized society were being pushed aside by men who did not hesitate to kill. One prominent citizen had been murdered, another pistol-whipped. Their stated intention was to do more of the same, to say nothing of Jim Yount's plan to marry Ruth, and his implication had been that it was simply a means to seize her land. Once they had won what they wished, there was no reason to believe the violence would cease. Gangrene had infected the area, and the only solution open to Ward McQueen was to amputate.

Yet he was no fool. He knew something of the gun skills of the men he would face. Even if he was killed himself, he must eliminate them. The townspeople could take care of such as Hollier and Packer. If he succeeded, Kim Sartain could handle the rest of it, and would. That was Kim's way.

Mounting the buckskin, he started down the trail toward Mannerhouse, only a few miles away. When he had ridden but a few hundred yards, he saw from his vantage point above the ranch that three riders were also headed for town. Jim Yount, Ruth, and, a few yards behind, Red Lund.

Pete Dodson, riding a sorrel horse, was also headed for town but by another route. Jim Yount was taking no chances.

* * * * *

The dusty main street of Mannerhouse lay warm under the morning sun. On the steps of the express office, the young rider, Rip, was sunning himself. In the saloon, Abel, behind his bar, watched nervously both his window and his door. He was on edge and aware, aware as a wild animal is when a strange creature nears its lair. Trouble was in the wind.

Gelvin's store was closed, unusual for this time of day. Abel glanced at Rip, and his brow furrowed. Rip was wearing two tied-down guns this morning, unusual for him.

Abel finished polishing a glass and put it down, glancing nervously at Packer. Suddenly Packer downed the drink and got to his feet. Walking to the door, he glanced up and down the street. All was quiet, yet the big man was worried. A man left the post office and walked along the boardwalk to the barbershop and entered. The sound of the closing door was the only sound. A hen pecked at something in the mouth of the alley near Gelvin's store. As he watched, he saw Pete Dodson stop his horse behind Gelvin's. Pete was carrying a rifle. Packer glanced over at Rip, noting the guns.

Packer turned suddenly, glaring at Abel. "Give me that scatter-gun you got under the bar!"

"Huh?" Abel was frightened. "I ain't got …"

"Don't give me that! I want that gun!"

There was an instant when Abel considered covering Packer or even shooting him, but the big man frightened him, and he put the shotgun on the bar. Packer picked it up and tiptoed to the window and put the gun down beside it. Careful to make no sound, he eased the window up a few inches. His position now covered Rip's side and back.

Abel cringed at what he had done. He liked Rip. The lean, easygoing, friendly young man might now be killed because of him. He'd been a coward. He should have refused, covered Packer, and called Rip inside. And he could have done that, if he wasn't such a coward. Now, because of him, a good man might be murdered, shot in the back. What was going on, anyway? This had been such a quiet little town.

Jim Yount rode up the street with Ruth beside him. Her face was pale and strained, and her eyes seemed unnaturally large.

Red Lund trailed a few yards behind. He drew up and tied his horse across the street.

From the saloon Abel could see it all. Jim Yount and Ruth Kermitt were approaching Rip from the west. North and west was Red Lund. Due north and in the shadow of Gelvin's was Pete Dodson. In the saloon was Packer. Rip was very neatly boxed, signed, and sealed. All but delivered.

Jim Keane, Logan's much older brother, was the express agent. He saw Jim Yount come, saw Red Lund across the street.

Rip got up lazily, smiling at Ruth.

"Come for your package, Miss Kermitt?" he asked politely. "While you're here, would you mind answering some questions."

"By whose authority?" Yount demanded sharply.

Ward McQueen, crouched behind the saloon, heard the reply clearly.

"The state of Texas, Yount," Rip replied. "I'm a Texas Ranger."

Jim Yount's short laugh held no humor. "This ain't Texas, and she answers no questions."

Ward McQueen opened the back door of the saloon and stepped inside.

Packer, intent on the scene before him, heard the door open. Startled and angry, he whirled around. Ward McQueen, who he had buried, was standing just inside the door. The shotgun was resting on the windowsill behind Rip. Packer went for his six-gun, but even as he reached, he knew it was hopeless. He saw the stab of flame, felt the solid blow of the bullet, and felt his knees turn to butter under him. He pitched forward on his face.

Outside, all hell broke loose. Ruth Kermitt, seeing Rip's situation, spurred her horse to bump Yount's, throwing him out of position. Instantly, she slid from the saddle and threw herself to the ground near the edge of the walk.

All seemed to have begun firing at once. Yount, cursing bitterly, fired at Rip. He in turn was firing at Red Lund. Ward stepped suddenly from the saloon and saw himself facing Yount, who had brought his mount under control. He fired at Yount, and a bullet from Dodson's rifle knocked splinters from the post in front of his face.

Yount's gun was coming into line, and McQueen fired an instant sooner. Yount fired, and they both missed. Ward's second shot hit Yount, who grabbed for the pommel. Ward walked a step forward, but something hit him, and he went to his knee. Red Lund loomed from somewhere, and Ward got off another shot. Lund's face was covered with blood.

There was firing from the stage station and from Gelvin's store. There was a thunder of hoofs, and a bloodred horse came charging down the street, its rider hung low like an Indian, shooting under the horse's neck.

Yount was down, crawling on his belly in the dust. He had lost hold of his six-shooter, but his right hand held a knife, and he was crawling toward Ruth. McQueen's six-shooter clicked on an empty chamber. How many shots were left in his other gun? He lifted it with his left hand. Something was suddenly wrong with his right. He rarely shot with his left hand, but now …

Yount was closer. Ruth was staring across the street, unaware. McQueen shot past Ruth, squeezing off the shot with his left hand. He saw Yount contract sharply as the bullet struck. McQueen fired again, and the gambler rolled over on his side, and the knife slipped from his fingers.

Abel ran from the saloon with a shotgun, and Gelvin from his store with a rifle. Then Ruth was running toward him, and he saw Kim Sartain coming back up the street, walking the red horse. Ward tried to rise to meet Ruth, but his knees gave way, and he went over on his face, thinking how weak she must think him. He started to rise again and blacked out.

* * * * *

When he could see again, Ruth was beside him. Kim was squatting on his heels. "Come on, Ward!" he said. "You've only been hit twice and neither of 'em bad. Can't you handle lead anymore?"

"What happened?"

"Clean sweep, looks like. Charlie Quayle got to us, and we hightailed it to the ranch. Hollier wanted to give us trouble, but we smoked him out. I believe there were others around, but if there were, they skipped the country. Whilst they were cleanin' up, I took it on the run for town. Halfway here, I thought I heard a shot, and when I hit the street, everybody in town was shootin', or that's what it looked like. Reg'lar Fourth of July celebration! Pete Dodson is dead, and Red Lund's dying with four bullets in him. Yount's alive, but he won't make it, either. Packer's dead."

Ward's head was aching, and he felt weak and sick, but he did not want to move, even to get out of the street. He just wanted to sit, to forget all that had taken place. With fumbling fingers, from long habit, he started to reload his pistols. Oddly, he found one of them contained three live shells. Somehow he must have reloaded, but he had no memory of it.

Rip came over. "My name's Coker, Ward. I couldn't figure any way to bust up Yount's operation without getting Ruth Kermitt away from him first, so I faked that package to get them into town, hoping I could get her away from them. I didn't figure they'd gang up on me like they did."

They helped Ward up and into the saloon. Gelvin brought

the doctor in. "Yount just died," Gelvin said, "cussing you and everybody concerned."

He sat back in a chair while the doctor patched him up. Again he had lost blood. "I've got to find a bed," he said to Kim. "There must be a hotel in town."

"You're coming back to the ranch," Ruth said. "We need you there. They told me you left me, Ward. Jim Yount said you pulled out and Kim with you. I hadn't seen him, and Yount said he'd manage the ranch until I found someone. Then he brought his own men in and fired Kim, who I hadn't seen, and I was surrounded and scared. If you had been there, or if I'd even known you were around, I …"

"Don't worry about it." Ward leaned his head back. All he wanted was rest.

Baldy Jackson helped him into a buckboard, Bud Fox driving. "You know that old brindle longhorn who turned up missin'? Well, I found him. He's got about thirty head with him, holed up in the prettiest little valley you ever did see. Looks like he's there to stay."

"He's like me," Ward commented, "so used to his range, he wouldn't be happy anywhere else."

"Then why think of anywhere else?" Ruth said. "I want you to stay."

FOUR CARD DRAW

When a man drew four cards, he could expect something like this to happen. Ben Taylor had probably been right when he told him his luck had run out. Despite that, he had a place of his own, and, come what may, he was going to keep it.

Nor was there any fault to find with the place. From the moment Allen Ring rode his claybank into the valley, he knew he was coming home. This was it; this was the place. Here he would stop. He'd been tumbleweeding all over the West now for ten years, and it was time he stopped, if he ever did, and this looked like his fence corner.

Even the cabin looked good, although Taylor told him the place had been empty for three years. It looked solid and fit, and while the grass was waist high all over the valley and up around the house, he could see trails through it, some of them made by unshod ponies—that meant wild horses—and some by deer. Then there were the tracks of a single shod horse, always the same one.

Those tracks always led right up to the door, and they stopped there; yet he could see that somebody with mighty small feet had been walking up to peer into the windows. Why would a person want to look into a window more than once? The window of an empty cabin? He had gone up and looked in himself, and all he saw was a dusty, dark interior with a ray of light from the opposite window, a table, a couple of chairs, and a fine old fireplace that had been built by skilled hands.

"You never built that fireplace, Ben Taylor," Ring had muttered, "you who never could handle anything but a running iron or a deck of cards. You never built anything in your life as fine and useful as that."

The cabin sat on a low ledge of grass backed up against the towering cliff of red rock, and the spring was not more than fifty feet away, a stream that came out of the rock and trickled pleasantly into a small basin before spilling out and winding thoughtfully down the valley to join a larger stream, a quarter of a mile away.

There were some tall spruces around the cabin and a couple of sycamores and a cottonwood near the spring. Some gooseberry bushes, too, and a couple of apple trees. The trees had been pruned.

"And you never did that, either, Ben Taylor," Allen Ring had said soberly. "I wish I knew more about this place."

Time had fled like a scared antelope, and with the scythe he found in the pole barn, he cut off the tall grass around the house, patched up the holes in the cabin where the pack rats had got in, and even thinned out the bushes—it had been several years since they had been touched—and repaired the pole barn.

The day he picked to clean out the spring was the day Gail Truman rode up to the house. He had been putting the finishing touches on a chair bottom he was making when he heard a horse's hoof strike stone, and he straightened up to see the girl sitting on the red pony. She was staring, open-mouthed, at the stacked hay from the grass he had cut and the washed windows of the house. He saw her swing down and run up to the window, and, dropping his tools, he strolled up.

"Hunting somebody, ma'am?"

She wheeled and stared at him, her wide blue eyes accusing. "What are you doing here?" she demanded. "What do you mean by moving in like this?"

He smiled, but he was puzzled, too. Ben Taylor had said nothing about a girl, especially a girl like this. "Why, I own the place?" he said. "I'm fixing it up so's I can live here."

"You own it?" Her voice was incredulous, agonized. "You couldn't own it! You couldn't. The man who owns this place is gone, and he would never sell it. Never!"

"He didn't exactly sell it, ma'am," Ring said gently. "He lost it to me in a poker game. That was down Texas way."

She was horrified. "In a poker game? Whit Bayly in a poker game? I don't believe it!"

"The man I won it from was called Ben Taylor, ma'am." Ring took the deed from his pocket and opened it. "Come to think of it, Ben did say that, if anybody asked about Whit Bayly, to say that he died down in the Guadeloupes … of lead poisoning."

"Whit Bayly is dead?" The girl looked stunned. "You're sure? Oh …"

Her face went white and still, and something in it seemed to die. She turned with a little gesture of despair and stared out across the valley, and his eyes followed hers. It was strange, Allen Ring told himself, but it was the first time he had looked just that way, and he stood there, caught up by something nameless, some haunting sense of the familiar.

Before him lay the tall grass of the valley, turning slightly now with the brown of autumn, and to his right a dark stand of spruce, standing stiffly, like soldiers on parade, and beyond them the swell of the hill, and farther to the right, the hill rolled up and stopped, and beyond lay a wider valley fading away into the vast purple and mauve of distance and here and there spotted with the golden candles of cottonwoods, their leaves bright yellow with nearing cold.

There was no word for this; it was a picture, yet a picture of which a man could only dream and never reproduce.

"It … it's beautiful, isn't it?" he said.

She turned on him, and for the first time, she seemed really to look at him, a tall young man with a shock of rust-brown hair and somber gray eyes, having about him the look of a rider and the look of a lonely man.

"Yes, it is beautiful. Oh, I've come here so many times to see it … the cabin, too. I think this is the loveliest place I have ever seen. I used to dream about …" She stopped, suddenly confused. "Oh, I'm sorry. I shouldn't talk so." She looked at him soberly. "I'd better go. I guess this is yours now."

He hesitated. "Ma'am," he said sincerely, "the place is mine, and, sure enough, I love it. I wouldn't swap this place for anything. But that view, that belongs to no man. It belongs to whoever looks at it with eyes to see it, so you come any time you like, and look all you please." Ring grinned. "Fact is," he said, "I'm aiming to fix the place up inside, and I'm sure no hand at such things. Maybe you could sort of help me. I'd like it kind of homey-like." He flushed. "You see, I sort of lived in bunkhouses all my life and never had no such place."

She smiled with a quick understanding and sympathy. "Of course! I'd love to, only …" Her face sobered. "… You won't be able to stay here. You haven't seen Ross Bilton yet, have you?"

"Who's he?" Ring asked curiously. He nodded toward the horsemen he saw approaching. "Is this the one?"

She turned quickly and nodded. "Be careful. He's the town marshal. The men with him are Ben Hagen and Stan Brule."

Brule he remembered—but would Brule remember him?

"By the way, my name is Allen Ring," he said, low-voiced.

"I'm Gail Truman. My father owns the Tall T brand."

Bilton was a big man with a white hat. Ring decided he didn't like him and that the feeling was going to be mutual. Brule he knew, so the stocky man was Ben Hagen. Brule had changed but little, some thinner, maybe, but his hatchet face as lean and poisonous as always.

"How are you, Gail?" Bilton said briefly. "Is this a friend of yours?"

Allen Ring liked to get his cards on the table. "Yes, a friend of hers, but also the owner of this place."

"You own Red Rock?" Bilton was incredulous. "That will be very hard to prove, my friend. Also, this place is under the custody of the law."

"Whose law?" Ring wanted to know. He was aware that Brule was watching him, wary but uncertain as yet.

"Mine. I'm the town marshal. There was a murder committed here, and until that murder is solved and the killer brought to justice, this place will not be touched. You have already seen fit to make changes, but perhaps the court will be lenient."

"You're the town marshal?" Allen Ring shoved his hat back on his head and reached for his tobacco. "That's mighty interesting. Howsoever, let me remind you that you're out of town right now."

"That makes no difference." Bilton's voice was sharp. Ring could see that he was not accustomed to being told off, that his orders were usually obeyed. "You will get off this place before nightfall."

"It makes a sight of difference to me," Allen replied calmly. "I bought this place by staking everything I had against it in a poker game. I drew four cards to win, a nine to match one I had and three aces. It was a fool play that paid off. I registered the deed. She's mine, legal. I know of no law that allows a place to be kept idle because there was a murder committed on it. If, after all this time, it hasn't been solved, I suggest the town get a new marshal."

Ross Bilton was angry, but he kept himself under control. "I've warned you, and you've been told to leave. If you do not leave, I'll use my authority to move you."

Ring smiled. "Now, listen, Bilton. You might pull that stuff on some folks that don't like trouble. You might bluff somebody into believing you had the authority to do this. You don't bluff me, and I simply don't scare … do I, Brule?"

He turned on Brule so sharply that the man stiffened in his saddle, his hand poised as though to grab for a gun. The half-breed's face stiffened with irritation, and then recognition came to him. "Allen Ring," he said. "You again."

"That's right, Brule. Only this time I'm not taking cattle through the Indian Nation. Not pushing them by that ratty bunch of rustlers and highbinders you rode with." Ring turned his eyes toward Bilton. "You're the law? And you ride with him? Why, the man's wanted in every county in Texas for everything from murder to horse thieving."

Ross Bilton stared at Ring for a long minute. "You've been warned," he said.

"And I'm staying," Ring replied sharply. "And keep your coyotes away if you come again. I don't like 'em."

Brule's fingers spread, and his lips stiffened with cold fury. Ring watched him calmly. "You know better than that, Brule. Wait until my back is turned. If you reach for a gun, I'll blow you out of your saddle."

Stan Brule slowly relaxed his hand and then wordlessly he

turned to follow Bilton and Hagan, who had watched with hard eyes.

Gail Truman was looking at him curiously. "Why, Brule was afraid of you!" she exclaimed. "Who are you, anyway?"

"Nobody, ma'am," he said simply. "I'm no gunfighter, just an hombre who ain't got brains enough to scare proper. Brule knows it. He knows he might beat me, but he knows I'd kill him. He was there when I killed a friend of his, Blaze Garden."

"But … but then you must be a gunman. Blaze Garden was a killer. I've heard Dad and the boys talk about him."

"No, I'm no gunman. Blaze beat me to the draw. In fact, he got off his first shot before my gun cleared the holster, only he shot too quick and missed. His second and third shots hit me while I was walking into him. The third shot wasn't so bad because I was holding my fire and getting close. He got scared and stepped back, and the fourth shot was too high. Then I shot, and I was close up to him then. One was enough. One is always enough if you place it right." He gestured at the place. "What's this all about? Mind telling me?"

"It's very simple, really. Nothing out here is very involved when you come to that. It seems that there's something out here that brings men to using guns much faster than in other places, and one thing stems from another. Whit Bayly owned this place. He was a fixing man, always tinkering and fixing things up. He was a tall, handsome man who all the girls loved …"

"You, too?" he asked quizzically.

She flushed. "Yes, I guess so, but I'm only eighteen now, and that was three, almost four years ago. I wasn't very pretty or very noticeable, and much too young. Sam Hazlitt was one of the richest men in the country around here, and Whit had a run-in with him over a horse. There had been a lot of stealing going on around, and Hazlitt traced some stock of his to this ranch, or so he claimed. Anyway, he accused Bayly of it, and Whit told him not to talk foolish. Furthermore, he told Hazlitt to stay off of his ranch. Well, folks were divided over who was in the right, but Whit had a lot of friends, and Hazlitt had four brothers and was clannish as all get-out.

"Not long after, some riders from Buck Hazlitt's ranch came by that way and saw a body lying in the yard, right over near the spring. When they came down to have a look, thinking Whit was hurt, they found Sam Hazlitt, and he'd been shot dead … in the back. They headed right for town, hunting Whit, and they found him. He denied it, and they were going to hang him, had a rope around his neck, and then I … I … well, I swore he wasn't anywhere near his ranch all day."

"It wasn't true?" Ring asked keenly, his eyes searching the girl's face. She avoided his eyes, flushing even more.

"Not … not exactly. But I knew he wasn't guilty. I just knew he wouldn't shoot a man in the back. I told them he was over to our place, talking with me, and he hadn't time to get back there and kill Sam. Folks didn't like it much. Some of them still believed he killed Sam, and some didn't like it because, despite the way I said it, they figured he was sparking a girl too young for him. I always said it wasn't that. As a matter of fact, I did see Whit over our way, but the rest of it was lies. Anyway, after a few weeks, Whit up and left the country."

"I see, and nobody knows yet who killed Sam Hazlitt?"

"Nobody. One thing that was never understood was what became of Sam's account book … sort of a tally book, but more than that. It was a sort of record he kept of a lot of things, and it was gone out of his pocket. Nobody ever found it, but they did find the pencil Sam used on the sand nearby. Dad always figured Sam lived long enough to write something, but that the killer stole the book and destroyed it."

"How about the hands? Could they have picked it up? Did Bilton question them about that?"

"Oh, Bilton wasn't marshal then. In fact, he was riding for Buck Hazlitt then. He was one of the hands who found Sam's body."

* * * * *

After the girl had gone, Allen Ring walked back to the house and thought the matter over. He had no intention of leaving. This was just the ranch he wanted, and he intended to live right here, yet the problem fascinated him. Living in the house and looking around the place had taught him a good deal about Whit Bayly. He was, as Gail had said, "a fixing man," for there were many marks of his handiwork aside from the beautifully made fireplace and the pruned apple trees. He was, Ring was willing to gamble, no murderer.

Taylor had said he died of lead poisoning. Who had killed Bayly? Why? Was it a casual shooting over some rangeland argument, or had he been followed from here by someone on vengeance bent? Or someone who thought he might know too much?

"You'll like the place." Taylor had said—that was an angle he hadn't considered before. Ben Taylor had actually seen this place himself! The more sign he read, the more tricky the trail became, and Allen walked outside and sat down against the cabin wall when his supper was finished, and lighted a smoke.

Stock had been followed to the ranch by Sam Hazlitt. If Whit was not the thief, then who was? Where had the stock been driven? He turned his eyes almost automatically toward the Mogollons, the logical place. His eyes narrowed, and he recalled that one night while playing cards, they had been talking of springs and water holes, and Ben Taylor had talked about Fossil Springs, a huge spring that roared thousands of gallons of water out of the earth.

"Place a man could run plenty of stock," he had said, and winked, "and nobody the wiser."

Those words had been spoken far away and long ago, and the Red Rock Ranch had not yet been put on the table; that was months later. There was, he recalled, a Fossil Creek somewhere north of here. And Fossil Creek might flow from Fossil Springs—perhaps Ben Taylor had talked more to effect than he knew. That had been Texas, and this was Arizona, and a casual bunkhouse conversation probably seemed harmless enough.

"We'll see, Ben," Ring muttered grimly. "We'll see."

Ross Bilton had been one of the Hazlitt hands at the time of the killing, one of the first on the scene. Now he was town marshal but interested in keeping the ranch unoccupied—why? None of it made sense, yet actually it was no business of his. Allen Ring thought that over and decided it was his business in a sense. He now owned the place and lived on it. If an old murder was to interfere with his living there, it behooved him to know the facts. It was a slight excuse for his curiosity.

Morning came, and the day drew on toward noon, and there was no sign of Bilton or Brule. Ring had loaded his rifle and kept it close to hand, and he was wearing two guns, thinking he might need a loaded spare, although he rarely wore more than one. Also, inside the cabin door, he had his double-barreled shotgun.

The spring drew his attention. At the moment he did not wish to leave the vicinity of the cabin, and that meant it was a good time to clean out the spring. Not that it needed it, but there were loose stones in the bottom of the basin and some moss. With this removed, he would have more water and clearer water. With a wary eye toward the canyon mouth, he began his work.

The sound of an approaching horse drew him erect. His rifle stood against the rocks at hand, and his guns were ready, yet, as the rider came into sight, he saw there was only one man, a stranger. He rode a fine bay gelding, and he was not a young man, but thick and heavy with drooping mustache and kind blue eyes. He drew up.

"Howdy," he said affably, yet taking a quick glance around before looking again at Ring. "I'm Rolly Truman, Gail's father."

"It's a pleasure," Ring said, wiping his wet hands on a red bandanna. "Nice to know the neighbors." He nodded at the spring. "I picked me a job. That hole's deeper than it looks."

"Good flow of water," Truman agreed. He chewed his mustache thoughtfully. "I like to see a young man with get-up about him, startin' his own spread, willin' to work."

Allen Ring waited. The man was building up to something; what, he knew not. It came then, carefully at first, yet shaping a loop as it drew near. "Not much range here, of course," Truman added. "You should have more graze. Ever been over in Cedar Basin? Or up along the East Verde bottom? Wonderful land up there, still some wild, but a country where a man could really do something with a few white-faced cattle."

"No, I haven't seen it," Ring replied, "but I'm satisfied. I'm not land hungry. All I want is a small piece, and this suits me fine."

Truman shifted in his saddle and looked uncomfortable. "Fact is, son, you're upsetting a lot of folks by being here. What you should do is move."

"I'm sorry," Ring said flatly. "I don't want to make enemies, but I won this place on a four card draw. Maybe I'm a fatalist, but somehow or other I think I should stick here. No man's got a right to think he can draw four cards and win anything, but I did, and in a plenty rough game. I had everything I owned in that pot. Now I got the place."

The rancher sat his horse uneasily, and then he shook his head. "Son, you've sure got to move. There's no trouble here now, but if you stay, she's liable to open old sores and start more trouble than any of us can stop. Besides, how did Ben Taylor get title to this place? Bayly had no love for him. I doubt if your title will stand up in court."

"As to that I don't know," Ring persisted stubbornly. "I have a deed that's legal enough, and I've registered that deed and my brand along with it. I did find out that Bayly had no heirs. So I reckon I'll sit tight until somebody comes along with a better legal claim than mine."

Truman ran his hand over his brow. "Well, I guess I don't blame you much, son. Maybe I shouldn't have come over, but I know Ross Bilton and his crowd, and I reckon I wanted to save myself some trouble as well as you. Gail, she thinks you're a fine young man. In fact, you're the first man she's ever showed interest in since Whit left, and she was a youngster then. It was a sort of hero worship she had for him. I don't want trouble."

Allen Ring leaned on the shovel and looked up at the older man. "Truman," he said, "are you sure you aren't buying trouble by trying to avoid it? Just what's your stake in this?"

The rancher sat very still, his face drawn and pale. Then he got down from his horse and sat on a rock. Removing his hat, he mopped his brow.

"Son," he said slowly, "I reckon I got to trust you. You've heard of the Hazlitts. They are a hard, clannish bunch, men who've lived by the gun most of their lives. Sam was murdered. Folks all know that when they find out who murdered him and why, there's goin' to be plenty of trouble around here. Plenty."

"Did you kill him?"

Truman jerked his head up. "No! No, you mustn't get that idea, but … well, you know how small ranchers are. There was a sight of rustlin' them days, and the Hazlitts were the big outfit. They lost cows."

"And some of them got your brand?" Ring asked shrewdly.

Truman nodded. "I reckon. Not so many, though. And not only me. Don't get me wrong, I'm not beggin' off the blame. Part of it is mine, all right, but I didn't get many. Eight or ten of us hereabouts slapped brands on Hazlitt stock … and at least five of us have the biggest brands around here now, some as big almost as the Hazlitts'."

Allen Ring studied the skyline thoughtfully. It was an old story and one often repeated in the West. When the War Between the States ended, men came home to Texas and the Southwest to find cattle running in thousands, unbranded and unowned. The first man to slap on a brand was the owner, with no way he could be contested.

Many men grew rich with nothing more than a wide loop and a running iron. Then the unbranded cattle were gone, the ranches had settled into going concerns, and the great days of casual branding had ended, yet there was still free range, and a man with that same loop and running iron could still build a herd fast.

More than one of the biggest ranchers had begun that way, and many of them continued to brand loose stock wherever found. No doubt that had been true here, and these men like Rolly Truman, good, able men who had fought Indians and built their homes to last, had begun just that way. Now the range was mostly fenced, and ranches had narrowed somewhat, but Ring could see what it might mean to open an old sore now.

Sam Hazlitt had been trailing rustlers—he had found out who they were and where the herds were taken, and he had been shot down from behind. The catch was that the tally book, with his records, was still missing. That tally book might contain evidence as to the rustling done by men who were now pillars of the community and open them to the vengeance of the Hazlitt outfit.

Often Western men threw a blanket over a situation. If a rustler had killed Sam, then all the rustlers involved would be equally guilty. Anyone who lived on this ranch might stumble on that tally book and throw the range into a bloody gun war in which many men now beyond the errors of their youth, with homes, families, and different customs, would die.

It could serve no purpose to blow the lid off the trouble now, yet Allen Ring had a hunch. In their fear of trouble for themselves, they might be concealing an even greater crime, aiding a murderer in his escape. There were lines of care in the face of Rolly Truman that a settled, established rancher should not have.

"Sorry," Ring said, "I'm staying. I like this place."

* * * * *

All through the noon hour, the tension was building. The air was warm and sultry, and there was a thickening haze over the mountains. There was that hot thickness in the air that presaged a storm. When he left his coffee to return to work, Ring saw three horsemen coming into the canyon mouth at a running walk. He stopped in the door and touched his lips with his tongue.

They reined up at the door, three hard-bitten, hard-eyed men with rifles across their saddlebows. Men with guns in their holsters and men of a kind that would never turn from trouble. These were men with the bark on, lean fanatics with lips thinned with old bitterness.

The older man spoke first. "Ring, I've heard about you. I'm Buck Hazlitt. These are my brothers, Joe and Dolph. There's talk around that you aim to stay on this place. There's been talk for years that Sam hid his tally book here. We figure the killer got that book and burned it. Maybe he did, and, again, maybe not. We want that book. If you want to stay on this place, you stay. But if you find that book, you bring it to us."

Ring looked from one to the other, and he could see the picture clearly. With men like these, hard and unforgiving, it was no wonder Rolly Truman and the other ranchers were worried. The years and prosperity had eased Rolly and his like into comfort and softness, but not these. The Hazlitts were of feudal blood and background.

"Hazlitt," Ring said, "I know how you feel. You lost a brother, and that means something, but if that book is still around, which I doubt, and I find it, I'll decide what to do with it all by myself. I don't aim to start a range war. Maybe there's some things best forgotten. The man who murdered Sam Hazlitt ought to pay."

"We'll handle that," Dolph put in grimly. "You find that book, you bring it to us. If you don't ..." His eyes hardened. "Well, we'd have to class you with the crooks."

Ring's eyes shifted to Dolph. "Class if you want," he flared. "I'll do what seems best to me with that book. But all of you folks are plumb proddy over that tally book. Chances are nine out of ten the killer found it and destroyed it."

"I don't reckon he did," Buck said coldly, "because we know he's been back here, a-huntin' it. Him an' his girl."

Ring stiffened. "You mean ...?"

"What we mean is our figger, not yours." Buck Hazlitt reined his horse around. "You been told. You bring that book to us. You try to buck the Hazlitts and you won't stay in this country."

Ring had his back up. Despite himself, he felt cold anger mounting within him. "Put this in your pipe, friend," he said harshly. "I came here to stay. No Hazlitt will change that. I ain't hunting trouble, but if you bring trouble to me, I'll handle it. I can bury a Hazlitt as easy as any other man."

Not one of them condescended to notice the remark. Turning their horses, they walked them down the canyon and out of it into the sultry afternoon.

Allen Ring mopped the sweat from his face and listened to the deep rumbling of far-off thunder, growling among the canyons like a grizzly with a toothache. It was going to rain. Sure as shooting, it was going to rain—a regular gully washer.

There was yet time to finish the job on the spring, so he picked up his shovel and started back for the job. The rock basin was nearly cleaned, and he finished removing the few rocks and the moss that had gathered. Then he opened the escape channel a little more to insure a more rapid emptying and filling process in the basin into which the trickle of water fell.

The water emerged from a crack in the rocks and trickled into the basin, and, finishing his job, Ring glanced thoughtfully to see if anything remained undone. There was still some moss on the rocks from which the water flowed, and, kneeling down, he leaned over to scrape it away. Pulling away the last shreds, he noticed a space from which a rock had recently fallen. Pulling more moss away, he dislodged another rock, and there, pushed into a niche, was a small black book!

Sam Hazlitt, dying, had evidently managed to shove it back in this crack in the rocks, hoping it would be found by someone not the killer.

Sitting back on his haunches, Ring opened the faded, canvas-bound book. A flap crossed over the page ends, and the book had been closed by a small tongue that slid into a loop of the canvas cover. Opening the book, he saw the pages were stained but still legible.

The next instant he was struck by lightning. At least, that was what seemed to happen. Thunder crashed, and something struck him on the skull, and he tried to rise, and something struck again. He felt a drop of rain on his face, and his eyes opened wide, and then another blow caught him, and he faded out into darkness, his fingers clawing at the grass to keep from slipping down into that velvety, smothering blackness.

* * * * *

He was wet. He turned a little, lying there, thinking he must have left a window open and the rain was ... His eyes opened, and he felt rain pounding on his face, and he stared, not at a boot with a California spur, but at dead brown grass, soaked with rain now, and the glistening smoothness of water-worn stones. He was soaked to the hide.

Struggling to his knees, he looked around, his head heavy, his lips and tongue thick. He blinked at a gray, rain-slanted world and at low gray clouds and a distant rumble of thunder following a streak of lightning along the mountaintops.

Lurching to his feet, he stumbled toward the cabin and pitched over the doorsill to the floor. Struggling again to his feet, he got the door closed, and in a vague, misty half-world of consciousness, he struggled out of his clothes and got his hands on a rough towel and fumblingly dried himself.

He did not think. He was acting purely from vague instinctive realization of what he must do. He dressed again, in dry clothes, and dropped at the table. After a while he sat up, and it was dark, and he knew he had blacked out again. He lighted a light and nearly dropped it to the floor. Then he stumbled to the washbasin and splashed his face with cold water. Then he bathed his scalp, feeling tenderly of the lacerations there.

A boot with a California spur. That was all he had seen. The tally book was gone, and a man wearing a new boot with a California-type spur, a large rowel, had taken it. He got coffee on, and, while he waited for it, he took his guns out and dried them painstakingly, wiping off each shell and then replacing them in his belt with other shells from a box on a shelf.

He reloaded the guns, and then, slipping into his slicker, he went outside for his rifle. Between sips of coffee, he worked over his rifle until he was satisfied. Then he threw a small pack together and stuffed his slicker pockets with shotgun shells.

The shotgun was an express gun and short-barreled. He slung it from a loop under the slicker. Then he took a lantern and went to the stable and saddled the claybank. Leading the horse outside into the driving rain, he swung into the saddle and turned along the road toward Basin.

There was no let-up in the rain. It fell steadily and heavily, yet the claybank slogged along, alternating between a shambling trot and a fast walk. Allen Ring, his chin sunk in the upturned collar of his slicker, watched the drops fall from the brim of his Stetson and felt the bump of the shotgun under his coat.

He had seen little of the tally book, but sufficient to know that it would blow the lid off the very range war they were fearing. Knowing the Hazlitts, he knew they would bring fire and gunplay to every home even remotely connected with the death of their brother.

The horse slid down a steep bank and shambled across the wide wash. Suddenly, the distant roar that had been in his ears for some time sprang into consciousness, and he jerked his head up. His horse snorted in alarm, and Ring stared, open-mouthed, at the wall of water, towering all of ten feet high, that was rolling down the wash toward him.

With a shrill Rebel yell, he slapped the spurs to the claybank, and the startled horse turned loose with an astounded leap and hit the ground in a dead run. There was no time to slow for the bank of the wash, and the horse went up, slipped at the very brink, and started to fall back.

Ring hit the ground with both boots and scrambled over the brink, and even as the flood roared down upon them, he heaved on the bridle, and the horse cleared the edge and stood, trembling. Swearing softly, Ring kicked the mud from his boots and mounted again. Leaving the raging torrent behind him, he rode on.

* * * * *

Thick blackness of night and heavy clouds lay upon the town when he sloped down the main street and headed the horse toward the barn. He swung down and handed the bridle to the liveryman.

"Rub him down," he said. "I'll be back."

He started for the doors and then stopped, staring at the three horses in neighboring stalls. The liveryman noticed his glance and looked at him.

"The Hazlitts. They come in about an hour ago, ugly as sin."

Allen Ring stood, wide-legged, staring grimly out the door. There was a coolness inside him now that he recognized. He dried his hands carefully.

"Bilton in town?" he asked.

"Sure is. Playin' cards over to the Mazatzal Saloon."

"He wear Mex spurs? Big rowels?"

The man rubbed his jaw. "I don't remember. I don't know at all. You watch out," he warned. "Folks are on the prod."

Ring stepped out into the street and slogged through the mud to the edge of the boardwalk before the darkened general store. He kicked the mud from his boots and dried his hands again, after carefully unbuttoning his slicker.

Nobody would have a second chance after this. He knew well enough that his walking into the Mazatzal would precipitate an explosion. Only he wanted to light the fuse himself, in his own way.

He stood there in the darkness alone, thinking it over. They would all be there. It would be like tossing a match into a lot of fused dynamite. He wished then that he was a better man with a gun than he was, or that he had someone to side him in this, but he had always acted alone and would scarcely know how to act with anyone else.

He walked along the boardwalk with long strides, his boots making hard sounds under the steady roar of the rain. He couldn't place that spur, that boot. Yet he had to. He had to get his hands on that book.

Four horses stood, heads down in the rain, saddles covered with slickers. He looked at them and saw they were of three different brands. The window of the Mazatzal was rain wet, yet standing at one side he glanced within.

The long room was crowded and smoky. Men lined the bar, feet on the brass rail. A dozen tables were crowded with card players. Everyone seemed to have taken refuge here from the rain. Picking out the Hazlitt boys, Ring saw them gathered together at the back end of the room. Then he got Ross Bilton pegged. He was at a table, playing cards, facing the door. Stan Brule was at this end of the bar, and Hagen was at a table against the wall, the three of them making three points of a flat triangle whose base was the door.

It was no accident. Bilton, then, expected trouble, and he was not looking toward the Hazlitts. Yet, on reflection, Ring could see the triangle could center fire from three directions on the Hazlitts as well. There was a man with his back to the door who sat in the game with Bilton. And not far from Hagen, Rolly Truman was at the bar.

Truman was toying with his drink, just killing time. Everybody seemed to be waiting for something. Could it be he they waited upon? No, that was scarcely to be considered. They could not know he had found the book, although it was certain at least one man in the room knew, and possibly others. Maybe it was just the tension, the building up of feeling over his taking over of the place at Red Rock. Allen Ring carefully turned down the collar of his slicker and wiped his hands dry again.

He felt jumpy and could feel that dryness in his mouth that always came on him at times like this. He touched his gun butts and then stepped over and opened the door.

Everyone looked up or around at once. Ross Bilton held a card aloft, and his hand froze at the act of dealing, holding still for a full ten seconds while Ring closed the door. He surveyed the room again and saw Ross play the card and say something in an undertone to the man opposite him. The man turned his head slightly, and it was Ben Taylor!

The gambler looked around, his face coldly curious, and for an instant their eyes met across the room, and then Allen Ring started toward him.

There was no other sound in the room, although they could all hear the unceasing roar of the rain on the roof. Ring saw something leap up in Taylor's eyes, and his own took on a sardonic glint.

"That was a good hand you dealt me down Texas way," Ring said. "A good hand!"

"You'd better draw more cards," Taylor said. "You're holdin' a small pair."

Ring's eyes shifted as the man turned slightly. It was the jingle of his spurs that drew his eyes, and there they were, the large rowelled California-style spurs, not common here. He stopped beside Taylor so the man had to tilt his head back to look up. Ring was acutely conscious that he was now centered between the fire of Brule and Hagen. The Hazlitts looked on curiously, uncertain as to what was happening.

"Give it to me, Taylor," Ring said quietly. "Give it to me now."

There was ice in his voice, and Taylor, aware of the awkwardness of his position, got to his feet, inches away from Ring.

"I don't know what you're talking about," he flared.

"No?"

Ring was standing with his feet apart a little, and his hands were breast high, one of them clutching the edge of his raincoat. He hooked with his left from that position, and the blow was too short, too sudden, and too fast for Ben Taylor.

The crack of it on the angle of his jaw was audible, and then Ring's right came up in the gambler's solar plexus, and the man's knees sagged. Spinning him around, Ring ripped open his coat with a jerk that scattered buttons across the room. Then from an inside pocket, he jerked the tally book.

He saw the Hazlitts start at the same instant that Bilton sprang back from the chair, upsetting it.

"Get him!" Bilton roared. "Get him!"

Ring shoved Taylor hard into the table, upsetting it and causing Bilton to spring back to keep his balance, and at the same instant, Ring dropped to a half crouch and, turning left, he drew with a flash of speed and saw Brule's gun come up at almost the same instant, and then he fired!

Stan Brule was caught with his gun just level, and the bullet smashed him on the jaw. The tall man staggered, his face a mask of hatred and astonishment mingled, and then Ring fired again, doing a quick spring around with his knees bent, turning completely around in one leap, and firing as his feet hit the floor.

He felt Hagen's bullet smash into him, and he tottered. Then he fired coolly, and, swinging as he fired, he caught Bilton right over the belt buckle.

It was fast action, snapping, quick, yet deliberate. The four fired shots had taken less than three seconds.

Stepping back, he scooped the tally book from the floor where it had dropped and then pocketed it. Bilton was on the floor, coughing blood. Hagen had a broken right arm and was swearing in a thick, stunned voice. Stan Brule had drawn his last gun. He had been dead before he hit the floor.

The Hazlitts started forward with a lunge, and Allen Ring took another step backward, dropping his pistol and swinging the shotgun, still hanging from his shoulder, into firing position.

"Get back!" he said thickly. "Get back, or I'll kill the three of you! Back … back to where you stood!"

Their faces wolfish, the three stood, lean and dangerous, yet the shotgun brooked no refusal, and slowly, bitterly, and reluctantly, the three moved back, step by step.

Ring motioned with the shotgun. "All of you … along the wall!"

The men rose and moved back, their eyes on him, uncertain, wary, some of them frightened.

Allen Ring watched them go, feeling curiously light-headed and uncertain. He tried to frown away the pain from his throbbing skull, yet there was a pervading weakness from somewhere else.

"My gosh!" Rolly Truman said. "The man's been shot! He's bleeding!"

"Get back!" Ring said thickly.

His eyes shifted to the glowing potbellied stove, and he moved forward, the shotgun waist-high, his eyes on the men who stared at him, awed.

The sling held the gun level, his hand partly supporting it, a finger on the trigger. With his left hand, he opened the stove and then fumbled in his pocket.

Buck Hazlitt's eyes bulged. "No!" he roared. "No, you don't!"

He lunged forward, and Ring tipped the shotgun and fired a blast into the floor, inches ahead of Hazlitt's feet. The rancher stopped so suddenly, he almost fell, and the shotgun tipped to cover him.

"Back!" Ring said. He swayed on his feet. "Back!" He fished out the tally book and threw it into the flames.

Something like a sigh went through the crowd. They stared, awed as the flames seized hungrily at the opened book, curling around the leaves with hot fingers, turning them brown and then black and to ashes.

Half-hypnotized, the crowd watched. Then Ring's eyes swung to Hazlitt. "It was Ben Taylor killed him," he muttered. "Taylor, and Bilton was with him. He ... he saw it."

"We take your word for it?" Buck Hazlitt demanded furiously.

Allen Ring's eyes widened, and he seemed to gather himself. "You want to question it? You want to call me a liar?"

Hazlitt looked at him, touching his tongue to his lips. "No," he said. "I figured it was them."

"I told you true," Ring said, and then his legs seemed to fold up under him, and he went to the floor.

The crowd surged forward, and Rolly Truman stared at Buck as Hazlitt neared the stove. The big man stared into the flames for a minute. Then he closed the door.

"Good!" he said. "Good thing! It's been a torment, that book, like a cloud hangin' over us all!"

* * * * *

The sun was shining through the window when Gail Truman came to see him. He was sitting up in bed and feeling better. It was good to be back on the place again, for there was much to do. She came in, slapping her boots with her quirt and smiling.

"Feel better?" she asked brightly. "You certainly look better. You've shaved."

He grinned and rubbed his jaw. "I needed it. Almost two weeks in this bed. I must have been hit bad."

"You lost a lot of blood. It's lucky you've a strong heart."

"It ain't … isn't so strong anymore," he said. "I think it's grown mighty shaky here lately."

Gail blushed. "Oh? It has? Your nurse, I suppose?"

"She is pretty, isn't she?"

Gail looked up, alarmed. "You mean, you …?"

"No, honey," he said, "you."

"Oh." She looked at him and then looked down. "Well, I guess …"

"All right?"

She smiled then, suddenly and warmly. "All right."

"I had to ask you," he said. "We had to marry."

"Had to? Why?"

"People would talk, a young, lovely girl like you over at my place all the time … would they think you were looking at the view?"

"If they did," she replied quickly, "they'd be wrong."

"You're telling me?" he asked.

MISTAKES CAN KILL YOU

Ma Redlin looked up from the stove. "Where's Sam? He still out yonder?"

Johnny rubbed his palms on his chaps. "He ain't comin' to supper, Ma. He done rode off."

Pa and Elsa were watching him, and Johnny saw the hard lines of temper around Pa's mouth and eyes. Ma glanced at him apprehensively, but when Pa did not speak, she looked to her cooking. Johnny walked around the table and sat down across from Elsa.

When Pa reached for the coffeepot, he looked over at Johnny. "Was he alone, boy? Or did he ride off with that no-account Albie Bower?"

It was in Johnny neither to lie nor to carry tales. Reluctantly, he replied: "He was with somebody. I reckon I couldn't be sure who it was."

Joe Redlin snorted and put down his cup. It was a sore point with Redlin that his son and only child, Sam, should take up with the likes of Albie Bower. Back in Pennsylvania and Ohio, the Redlins had been good, God-fearing folk, while Bower was no good and came from a no-good outfit. Lately he had been flashing money around, but he claimed to have won it gambling at Degner's Four Star Saloon.

"Once more I'll tell him," Redlin said harshly. "I'll have no son of mine traipsin' with that Four Star outfit. Pack of thieves, that's what they are."

Ma looked up worriedly. She was a buxom woman with a round apple-cheeked face. Good humor was her normal manner. "Don't you be sayin' that away from home, Joe Redlin. That Loss Degner is a gunslinger, and he'd like nothin' so much as to shoot you after you takin' Elsa from him."

"I ain't afeerd of him." Redlin's voice was flat. Johnny knew that what he said was true. Joe Redlin was not afraid of Degner, but he avoided him, for Redlin was a small rancher, a onetime farmer, and not a fighting man. Loss Degner was bad all through and made no secret of it. His Four Star was the hangout for all the tough element, and Degner had killed two men since Johnny had been in the country, as well as pistol-whipping a half dozen more.

It was not Johnny's place to comment, but secretly he knew Joe Redlin was right. Once he had even gone so far as to warn Sam, but it only made Sam angry.

Sam was almost twenty-one and Johnny but seventeen, but Sam's family had protected him, and he had lived always close to the competence of Pa Redlin. Johnny had been doing a man's work since he was thirteen, fighting a man's battles, and making his own way in a hard world.

Johnny also knew what only Elsa seemed to guess, that it was Hazel, Degner's red-haired singer, who drew Sam Redlin to the Four Star. It was rumored that she was Degner's woman, and Johnny had said as much to Sam. Sam had flown into a rage and, whirling on Johnny, had drawn back his fist. Something in Johnny's eyes stopped him, and, although Sam would never have admitted it, he was suddenly afraid.

Like Elsa, Johnny had been adrift when he came to the B Bar and was taken in. Half dead with pneumonia, he had come up to the door on his black gelding, and the Redlins' hospitality had given him a bed and the best care the frontier could provide, and, when Johnny was well, he went to work to repay them. Then he stayed on for the spring roundup as a forty-a-month hand.

He volunteered no information, and they asked him no questions. He was slightly built and below medium height, but broad-shouldered and wiry. His shock of chestnut hair always needed cutting, and his green eyes held a lurking humor. He moved with deceptive slowness, but he was quick at work, and skillful with his hands. Nor did he wait to be told about things, for even before he began riding, he had mended the buckboard, cleaned out and shored up the spring, repaired the door hinges, and cleaned all the guns.

"We collect from Walters tomorrow," Redlin said suddenly. "Then I'm goin' to make a payment on that Sprague place and put Sam on it. With his own place, he'll straighten up and go to work."

Johnny stared at his plate, his appetite gone. He knew what that meant, for it had been in Joe Redlin's mind that Sam should marry Elsa and settle on that place. Johnny looked up suddenly, and his throat tightened as he looked at her. The gray eyes caught his, searched them for an instant, and then moved away, and Johnny watched the lamplight in her ash blonde hair, turning it to old gold.

He pushed back from the table and excused himself, going out into the moonlit yard. He lived in a room he had built into a corner of the barn. They had objected at first, wanting him to stay at the house, but he could not bear being close to Elsa, and then he had the lonely man's feeling for seclusion. Actually it had other advantages, for it kept him near his horse, and he never knew when he might want to ride on.

That black gelding and his new .44 Winchester had been the only incongruous notes in his getup when he arrived at the B Bar, for he had hidden his guns and his best clothes in a cave up the mountain, riding down to the ranch in shabby range clothes with only the .44 Winchester for safety.

He had watched the ranch for several hours, despite his illness, before venturing down to the door. It paid to be careful, and there were men about who might know him.

Later, when securely in his own room, he had returned to his cache and dug out the guns and brought his outfit down to the ranch. Yet nobody had ever seen him with guns on, nor would they, if he was lucky.

The gelding turned its head and nickered at him, rolling its eyes at him. Johnny walked into the stall and stood there, one hand on the horse's neck. "Little bit longer, boy, then we'll go. You sit tight."

There was another reason why he should leave now, for he had learned from Sam that Flitch was in town. Flitch had been on the Gila during the fight, and he had been a friend of Card Wells, who Johnny had killed at Picacho. Moreover, Flitch had been in Cimarron a year before that when Johnny, only fifteen then, had evened the score with the men who had killed his father and stolen their outfit. Johnny had gunned two of them down and put the third into the hospital.

* * * * *

Johnny was already on the range when Sam Redlin rode away the next morning to make his collection. Pa Redlin rode out with Elsa and found Johnny branding a yearling. Pa waved and rode on, but Elsa sat on her horse and watched him. "You're a good hand, Johnny," she said when he released the calf. "You should have your own outfit."

"That's what I want most," he admitted. "But I reckon I'll never have it."

"You can if you want it enough. Is it because of what's behind you?"

He looked up quickly then. "What do you know of me?"

"Nothing, Johnny, but what you've told us. But once, when I started into the barn for eggs, you had your shirt off, and I saw those bullet scars. I know bullet scars, because my own father had them. And you've never told us anything, which usually means there's something you aren't anxious to tell."

"I guess you're right." He tightened the girth on his saddle. "There ain't much to tell, though. I come West with my pa, and he was a lunger. I drove the wagon myself after we left Independence. Clean to Caldwell, then on to Santa Fe. We got us a little outfit with what Pa had left, and some mean fellers stole it off us, and they killed Pa."

Joe Redlin rode back to join them as Johnny was swinging into the saddle. He turned and glanced down at the valley. "Reckon that range won't get much use, Johnny," he said anxiously, "and the stock sure need it. Fair to middlin' grass, but too far to water."

"That draw, now," Johnny suggested. "I've been thinkin' about that draw. It would take a sight of work, but a couple of good men with teams and some elbow grease could build them a dam across that draw. There's a sight of water comes down when it rains, enough to last most of the summer if it was dammed. Maybe even the whole year."

The three horses started walking toward the draw, and

Johnny pointed out what he meant. "A feller over to Mobeetie did that one time," he said, "and it washed his dam out twice, but the third time she held, and he had him a little lake all the year round."

"That's a good idea, Johnny." Redlin studied the setup and then nodded. "A right good idea."

"Sam and me could do it," Johnny suggested, avoiding Pa Redlin's eyes.

Pa Redlin said nothing, but both Johnny and Elsa knew that Sam was not exactly ambitious about extra work. He was a good hand, Sam was, strong and capable, but he was bigheaded about things and was little inclined to sticking with a job.

"Reminds me," Pa said, glancing at the sun. "Sam should be back soon."

"He might stop in town," Elsa suggested, and was immediately sorry she had said it, for she could see the instant worry on Redlin's face. The idea of Sam Redlin stopping at the Four Star with seven thousand on him was scarcely a pleasant one. Murder had been done there for much, much less. And then Sam was overconfident. He was even cocky.

"I reckon I'd better ride in and meet him, " Joe Redlin said, genuinely worried now. "Sam's a good boy, but he sets too much store by himself. He figures he can take care of himself anywhere, but that pack of wolves ..." His voice trailed off to silence.

Johnny turned in his saddle. "Why, I could just as well ride in," he said casually. "I ain't been to town for a spell, and if anything happened, I could lend a hand."

Pa Redlin was about to refuse, but Elsa spoke up quickly. "Let him go, Pa. He could do some things for me, too, and Johnny's got a way with folks. Chances are he could get Sam back without trouble."

That's right! Johnny's thoughts were grim. *Send me along to save your boy. You don't care if I get shot, just so's he's been saved. Well, all right, I'll go. When I come back, I'll climb my gelding and light out. Up to Oregon. I've never been to Oregon.*

Flitch was in town. His mouth tightened a little, but at that it would be better than Pa's going. Pa always said the wrong thing, being outspoken-like. He was a man who spoke his mind, and to speak one's mind to Flitch or Loss Degner would mean a shooting. It might be he could get Sam out of town all right. If he was drinking, it would be hard. Especially if that redhead had her hands on him.

"You reckon you could handle it?" Pa asked doubtfully.

"Sure," Johnny said, his voice a shade hard, "I can handle it. I doubt if Sam's in any trouble. Later, maybe. All he'd need is somebody to side him."

"Well," Pa was reluctant, "better take your Winchester. My six-gun, too."

"You hang onto it. I'll make out."

Johnny turned the gelding and started back toward the ranch, his eyes cold. Seventeen he might be, but four years on the frontier on your own make pretty much of a man out of you. He didn't want any more shooting, but he had six men dead on his back trail now, not counting Comanches and Kiowas. Six, and he was seventeen. Next thing, they would be comparing him to Billy the Kid or to Wes Hardin.

He wanted no gunfighter's name, only a little spread of his own where he could run a few cows and raise horses, good stock, like some he had seen in east Texas. No range ponies for him, but good blood. That Sprague place now … but that was Sam's place, or as good as his. Well, why not? Sam was getting Elsa, and it was little enough he could do for Pa and Ma, to bring Sam home safe.

He left the gelding at the water trough and walked into the

barn. In his room he dug some saddle gear away from a corner and, out of a hiding place in the corner, he took his guns. After a moment's thought, he took but one of them, leaving the .44 Russian behind. He didn't want to go parading into town with two guns on him, looking like a sure-enough shooter. Besides, with only one gun and the change in him, Flitch might not spot him at all.

Johnny was at the gate, riding out, when Elsa rode up. Elsa looked at him, her eyes falling to the gun on his hip. Her face was pale and her eyes large. "Be careful, Johnny. I had to say that, because you know how hotheaded Pa is. He'd get killed, and he might get Sam killed."

That was true enough, but Johnny was aggrieved. He looked her in the eyes. "Sure, that's true, but you didn't think of Sam, now, did you? You were just thinking of Pa."

Her lips parted to protest, but then her face seemed to stiffen. "No, Johnny, it wasn't only Pa I thought of. I did think of Sam. Why shouldn't I?"

That was plain enough. Why shouldn't she? Wasn't she going to marry him? Wasn't Sam getting the Sprague place when they got that money back safe?

He touched his horse lightly with a spur and moved on past her. All right, he would send Sam back to her, if he could. It was time he was moving on, anyway.

* * * * *

The gelding liked the feel of the trail and moved out fast. Ten miles was all, and he could do that easy enough, and so he did it, and Johnny turned the black horse into the street and stopped before the livery stable, swinging down. Sam's horse was tied at the Four Star's hitch rail. The saddlebags were gone.

Johnny studied the street and then crossed it and walked

down along the buildings on the same side as the Four Star. He turned quickly in at the door.

Sam Redlin was sitting at a table with the redhead, the saddlebags on the table before him, and he was drunk. He was very drunk. Johnny's eyes swept the room. The bartender and Loss Degner were standing together, talking. Neither of them paid any attention to Johnny, for neither knew him. But Flitch did.

Flitch was standing down the bar with Albie Bower, but none of the old Gila River outfit. Both of them looked up, and Flitch kept looking, never taking his eyes from Johnny. Something bothered him, and maybe it was the one gun.

Johnny moved over to Sam's table. They had to get out of here fast, before Flitch remembered.

"Hi, Sam," he said. "Just happened to be in town, and Pa said if I saw you to side you on the way home."

Sam stared at him sullenly. "Side me? You?" He snorted his contempt. "I need no man to side me. You can tell Pa I'll be home later tonight." He glanced at the redhead. "Much later."

"Want I should carry this stuff home for you?" Johnny put his hand on the saddlebags.

"Leave him be," Hazel, the redhead, protested angrily. "Can't you see he don't want to be bothered? He's capable of takin' care of himself, an' he don't need no kid for guardian."

"Beat it," Sam said. "You go on home. I'll come along later."

"Better come now, Sam." Johnny was getting worried, for Loss Degner had started for the table.

"Here, you." Degner was sharp. "Leave that man alone. He's a friend of mine, and I'll have no saddle tramp annoying my customers."

Johnny turned on him. "I'm no saddle tramp. I ride for his pa. He asked me to ride home with him … now. That's what I aim to do."

As he spoke, he was not thinking of Degner, but of Flitch. The gunman was behind him now, and neither Flitch, fast as he was, nor Albie Bower, was above shooting a man in the back.

"I said to beat it." Sam stared at him drunkenly. "Saddle tramp's what you are. Folks never should have took you in."

"That's it," Degner said. "Now get out. He don't want you nor your company."

There was a movement behind him, and he heard Flitch say: "Loss, let me have him. I know this hombre. This is that kid gunfighter, Johnny O'Day, from the Gila."

Johnny turned slowly, his green eyes flat and cold.

"Hello, Flitch. I heard you were around." Carefully he moved away from the table, aware of the startled look on Hazel's face, the suddenly tight awareness on the face of Loss Degner. "You lookin' for me, Flitch?" It was a chance he had to take. His best chance now. If shooting started he might grab the saddlebags and break for the door and then the ranch. They would be through with Sam Redlin once the money was gone.

"Yeah." Flitch stared at him, his unshaven face hard with the lines of evil and shadowed by the intent that rode him hard. "I'm lookin' for you. Always figured you got off easy … made you a fast rep gunnin' down your betters."

Bower had moved up beside him, but Loss Degner had drawn back to one side. Johnny's eyes never left Flitch. "You in this, Loss?"

Degner shrugged. "Why should I be? I was no Gila River gunman. This is your quarrel. Finish it between you."

"All right, Flitch," Johnny said. "You want it. I'm givin' you your chance to start the play."

The stillness of a hot midafternoon lay on the Four Star. A fly buzzed against the dusty, cobwebbed back window. Somewhere in the street, a horse stamped restlessly, and a distant pump creaked.

Flitch stared at him, his little eyes hard and bright. His sweat-stained shirt was torn at the shoulder, and there was dust ingrained in the pores of his face.

His hands dropped in a flashing draw, but he had only cleared leather when Johnny's first bullet hit him, puncturing the Bull Durham tag that hung from his shirt pocket. The second shot cut the edge of it, and the third, fourth, and fifth slammed into Albie Bower, knocking him back step by step, but Albie's gun was hammering, and it took the sixth shot to put him down.

Johnny stood over them, staring down at their bodies, and then he turned to face Loss Degner.

Degner was smiling, and he held a gun in his hand from which a thin tendril of smoke lifted. Startled, Johnny's eyes flickered to Sam Redlin.

Sam lay across the saddlebags, blood trickling from his temples. He had been shot through the head by Degner under cover of the gun battle, murdered without a chance!

Johnny O'Day's eyes lifted to Loss Degner's. The saloonkeeper was still smiling. "Yes, he's dead, and I've killed him. He had it coming, the fool. Thinking we cared to listen to his bragging. All we wanted was that money, and now we've got it. Me … Hazel and I. We've got it."

"Not yet." Johnny's lips were stiff and his heart was cold. He was thinking of Pa, Ma, and Elsa. "I'm still here."

"You?" Degner laughed. "With an empty gun? I counted your shots, boy. Even Johnny O'Day is cold turkey with an empty gun. Six shots … two for Flitch, and beautiful shooting, too, but four shots for Albie, who was moving and shooting, not so easy a target. But now I've got you. With you dead, I'll just say Sam came here without any money, that he got shot during the fight. Sound good to you?"

Johnny still faced him, his gun in his hand. "Not bad," he

said, "but you still have me here, Loss. And this gun ain't empty."

Degner's face tightened and then relaxed. "Not empty? I counted the shots, kid, so don't try bluffing me. Now I'm killing you." He tilted his gun toward Johnny O'Day, and Johnny fired once, twice ... a third time. As each bullet hit him, Loss Degner jerked and twisted, but the shock of the wounds, and death wounds they were, was nothing to the shock of the bullets from that empty gun.

He sagged against the bar and then slipped toward the floor.

Johnny moved in on him. "You can hear me, Loss?" The killer's eyes lifted to his. "This ain't a six-shooter. It's a Watch twelve-shot Navy gun, Thirty-Six caliber. She's right handy, Loss, and it only goes to show you shouldn't jump to conclusions."

Hazel sat at the table, staring at the dying Degner.

"You better go to him, Red," Johnny said quietly. "He's only got a minute."

She stared at him as he picked up the saddlebags and backed to the door.

Russell, the storekeeper, was on the steps with a half dozen others, none of whom he knew. "Degner killed Sam Redlin," he said. "Take care of Sam, will you?"

At Russell's nod, Johnny swung to the saddle and turned the gelding toward home.

He wouldn't leave now. He couldn't leave now. They would be all alone there, without Sam. Besides, Pa was going to need help on that dam. "Boy," he touched the gelding's neck, "I reckon we got to stick around for a while."

SHOWDOWN ON THE TUMBLING T

I

Under the slate gray sky, the distant mountains were like a heap of rusty scrap iron thrown helter-skelter along the far horizon. Nearby, the desert was the color of pink salmon and scattered with the gray of sagebrush and a few huddles of disconsolate greasewood. The only spot of green anywhere in sight was the sharp, strong green of tall pines in a notch of the rust-red mountains.

That was the place I'd come from Texas to find, the place where I was to hole up until Hugh Taylor could send word for me. It was something to have a friend like Hugh, someone to give you a hand up when the going was rough. When I had returned from Mexico to find myself a fugitive from justice, he had been the only one to offer help.

A few scattered drops of rain pounded dust from the desert. I dug into my pack for my slicker. By the time I had it on, the rain was coming down in a steady downpour that looked fair to last the night through as well as the afternoon.

Rowdy, my big black, was beginning to feel the hard going of the past weeks. It was the only time I had ever seen the big horse even close to weariness, and it was no wonder. We had come out of Dimmit County, Texas to the Apache country of central Arizona, and the trails had been rough.

The red rocks of the mountains began to take on form and line, and I could see the raw cancers of washes that ate into the face of the plain, and the deep scars of canyons. Here and there lines of gray or green climbed the creases in the rock, evidence of underlying water or frequent rains among the high peaks.

The trail curved north, skirting the mountains toward the sentinel pines. "Ride right to the Tin Cup Ranch," Hugh Taylor had said, "and when you get there, ask for Bill Keys. He'll be in charge, and he'll fix you up until this blows over. I'm sure I can get you cleared in a short time."

The mountains cracked wide open on my left, and the trail turned up a slope between the pines. Blue gentians carpeted both sides of the road and crept back under the trees in a solid mass of almost sky blue. The trail was faint and apparently used very little, but there were tracks made by two riders, and I watched them curiously. The tracks were fresh, and they were headed into the Tin Cup canyon.

You can bet I had my eyes open, for even so far away from anyone that knew me, there might be danger, and a man on the dodge learns to be careful.

Then I heard a shot.

It rapped out sharp and clear and final, bringing my head up with a jerk and my hand down to the stock of my Winchester. My rifle rode in a scabbard that canted back so that the stock almost touched my right thigh, and I could draw that rifle almost as fast as a man could draw a six-gun.

Rowdy heard that shot, too, and Rowdy knew what shooting could mean. He skirted the rocks that partially barred the way into the Tin Cup, and I looked down into a little valley with a stone barn and stone house, two corrals and two riderless horses.

Then I saw the men. The air was sharp and clear, and they were only a couple of hundred yards off. There were three of them, and one was lying on the ground. The man who stood over the body looked up and yelled at the other one near the corner of the house. "No, it ain't him!" And then they both saw me.

Panic must have hit them both, but one of them made a break for his horse while the other swung his hand down for his gun. Honest men don't start shooting when a stranger rides up, so, as his six-gun lifted, my rifle cleared the boot. He fired, but I wasn't worried. He was much too far away.

He made a dive for his horse, and I held my fire. As he settled in the saddle, I squeezed off my shot. He jerked like he was hit, and I saw the gun fall from his hand into the rocks, and then they were taking out of there, but fast. They wanted no part of my shooting.

Rowdy wasn't gun-shy. With me in the saddle, he had no cause to be, after all we had been through down Mexico way. That was a part of my life I never talked about much, and even Hugh, who was my best friend, knew nothing about it. To him I was still the quiet kid he had seen grow up on our uncle's ranch, the XY.

Rowdy was in no shape for a chase, so I let the riders go and swung down beside the old man and felt of his pulse. That was mostly a matter of form. No man with that last bullet hole where he had it was going to be alive. The first shot was a bit high, and I could see there had been some interval, for the blood around the first wound was coagulated.

A horse's hoof clicked on stone, and I turned with my hands spread. You don't pull anything fancy when four men are looking down rifles at you.

"What did you kill him for?" The speaker was a squat, broad-chested man with a square, red face and gimlet eyes.

He looked tough as a winter in the mountains, and at least two of the riders with him looked fit to side the devil on a ride through hell.

"Don't jump your fences, pardner," I told him, pretty chilly, "I didn't shoot this gent. When I rode into the Cup, two hombres were standing here, one right over him. They took a shot at me, then lit out, ridin' up the valley as I came in."

"We heard shootin'," the square-faced man replied. "He's dead, and you're here."

My eyes went over them, sizing them up. Nobody needed to burn any brands on this hide for me. Here I was on the dodge from one killing of which I wasn't guilty, and now I'd run smack dab into another. Nobody had seen those other riders but me, so what happened now depended a whole lot on just who and what these men were.

At first glance I could see there was only one man of the four who would give anybody a break. He was a young fellow with brown eyes and dark hair, and a careful look in his eyes. He looked smart and he looked honest, although a man can be fooled on both counts.

The square-built man who had done the talking seemed to be the big gee. "Who are you, anyway?" he demanded. "What brings you here?"

Something in the way he asked that question let me get downwind of an idea. "Why," I decided to tell this hombre nothing, least of all that I was Wat Bell, "they call me the Papago Kid, and I'm from down Sonora way.

"As for what brings me here, it was this black horse brought me, and the trail through the pines. A lot of trails have brought me a lot of places, and," I added this with some meaning, "when I wanted to ride out, nobody stopped me."

His eyes sharpened down, and his lips thinned out, and I

could see the old devil coming up in his eyes. This man was not one you could push far. He figured he was some salty, and he had no liking for being called up to the mark by any casual drifter. However, there was a funny little frown came into his eyes when I mentioned my name, and somehow the idea was there, full size and ready for branding, that he had expected another name. That feeling was so strong in me that it started me thinking about a lot of things.

Sometimes a man rides trails and reads sign so long that he develops an instinct for things. There was the strong smell of trouble in my nostrils now, and for some reason I knew that I'd made a good bet when I told him I was the Papago Kid. The funny part of it was that if he could find a way to check back down the Sonora trail, he'd find out I hadn't lied. A man sometimes can have two names that take separate trails, and if I was young Wat Bell in Dimmit County, Texas, I was also the Papago Kid down in Sonora.

"Lynch," the young fellow interrupted, "let's get in out of this rain, and get the body in, too. I liked old Simon Ludlow, and I don't like his body lying around like this." Then he added. "We can talk just as well over some coffee, anyway."

Lynch hesitated, still not liking me and itching for gunplay. "All right," he agreed, and turning to the other riders, a fat-faced man and a tall, stoop-shouldered rider, he added: "You two pick Ludlow's body up and cart it out to the stable. Cover it with a blanket, and then come on in. Better put the horses in, too." He looked at the tall man. "Don't leave anything undone, Bill," he added.

When I heard the tall man called Bill, a faint suspicion stirred in me, but I didn't look up. When I did, the fat man answered my question for me without any talking from me. "You take his feet, Keys, I'll get his shoulders."

Lynch turned abruptly toward the door of the stone house, and I followed with the young fellow behind me. Inside, Lynch got out of his slicker, and I got a shock. He was wearing a sheriff's badge on his vest.

"The coffee was your idea, Dolliver," Lynch suggested. "Want to start it?"

Dolliver nodded, and I knew he had seen my reaction to that badge and was curious about it. He turned toward the shelves and began taking things down as if he knew the place. In the meantime, I was trying to scout my trail and read the sign of this situation I'd run into.

Hugh Taylor had told me to ride to the Tin Cup and ask for Bill Keys. Yet when I arrived here, there was a dead man on the ground who isn't Bill Keys but is apparently the owner of the place. Meanwhile, Keys appears to be riding for the sheriff, and with what reason I had no idea.

It was a neat little house, tidy as an old maid's boudoir, and the smell of coffee that soon filled the room gave it a cozy, homelike feel. The fireplace was big enough, and all the cooking utensils were bright and clean. A blanket over a door curtained off an inner room.

Lynch dropped astride a chair and began to build a smoke. He had a bullethead covered with tight ringlets and a mustache that drooped in contrast. Slinging my hat on a hook, I hung up my own slicker and dropped into another chair. Lynch saw my two guns, and his face chilled a little. Something about me disturbed him, and I decided it was partly the guns—the fact that I was wearing them, not that he feared them.

"You call yourself the Papago Kid?" Lynch's question was sharp.

My eyes held his, and I knew Sheriff Lynch and I were not going to be friends. He was distinctly on the prod, but he was digging for something, too. I was beginning to wonder if I didn't know what it was he wanted.

"I've been called that," I said, "and I like the name. You can use it."

"Did you get a good look at those two riders who lit out of here? The two you said you saw?"

"I did see them. No, the look I got wasn't too good. One of them legged it for his bronc, and the other grabbed iron. Naturally, with a man drawing a gun on me, even at that distance, I wasn't wasting any time looking him over."

"How many shots did you hear?"

"One."

Dolliver turned around from the coffee. "I heard three."

"That's right," I agreed, "one shot apparently killed the old man, then I rounded into sight, and one of these hombres took a shot at me. I shot back." I hitched my chair back a little. "However, as you no doubt saw, the old man was shot twice. I figure he was wounded some place away from the ranch, then trailed down by the killers who finished the job."

"What gives you that idea?" Lynch demanded.

"If you noticed, Sheriff," I said, "the rain hadn't washed out the old man's tracks. Those tracks came from toward the corrals, and even from where I stood, I could see the old man had fallen down twice on that little slope, and there were blood spots on his clothes."

It was obvious enough that the sheriff had seen nothing of the kind, and he studied me carefully. I was doing some thinking on my own hook. The reason the sheriff hadn't seen those tracks was because all his attention had been centered on me.

Dolliver, whose attitude I liked, brought the coffee up to the table, filled our cups. He was a clean cut youngster and no fool.

The door opened then, and Bill Keys came in with his fat

friend. They knocked the rain from their hats and shed their slickers, both of them looking me over while they were doing it. Dolliver filled cups for them, and they found chairs and sat down.

It struck me as faintly curious that Sheriff Lynch was making no effort to trail the men I had mentioned, nor to see if there were tracks to back up my story. I wondered what Dolliver thought of that and was glad that he was with us. This was new country for me, and I was definitely in a bad spot, and unless the breaks came my way, I'd soon have the choice of shooting my way out or I'd find myself looking into my past through the leaves of a cottonwood with the loop end of a rope around my neck.

"You ever been in this country before?" Lynch demanded.

"Never. When I left my home in California, I crossed Arizona down close to Yuma and went into Mexico."

"How'd you happen to find this place? It ain't the easiest valley to find." He stared at me suspiciously, his eyes trying to pry behind my guileless eyes. I was wearing my most innocent face, carefully saved for just such emergencies.

"Did you ever cross that desert behind here?" I asked. "The only spot of green a man can see is right here. Naturally, I headed for the pines. Figured there might be people where there was water."

That was simple enough even for him, and he mulled over it a little. "You said you came from California? You sound like a Texan to me."

"Hell," I grinned cheerfully, "it's no wonder! On the last spread I rode for down Mexico way, there were eight Texans. My folks spoke Spanish around home," I lied, "so when I talked English with that Texas outfit, naturally I picked up their lingo."

The story was plausible enough, but Lynch didn't like it. He didn't get a chance to ask any more questions for a minute as I beat him to it. "What's up, Sheriff?" I asked. "Is this a posse? And if it is, why pick on me?"

Lynch didn't like that, and he didn't like me. "Huntin' a Texas outlaw supposed to be headed this way," he said, grudgingly, "a murderer named Wat Bell. We got word he was headed west, so we're cuttin' all the trails."

"Bad weather to be riding," I sympathized, "unless you're on a red hot trail. Is this Bell a bad hombre? Will it take four of you?"

Dolliver's eyes were shrewd and smiling. "I'm not one of them," he told me. "I have a little ranch just over the mountain from here, and joined these boys back in the pines when they headed this way. My ranch is the Tumbling T."

II

Lynch ended his questions and devoted himself to his coffee. From the desultory conversation that followed while Lynch mulled things over, I learned that the dead man, old Simon Ludlow, had owned the Tin Cup and had no enemies that anybody knew. Win Dolliver was his nearest neighbor and liked the old man very much, as had his sister, Maggie Dolliver.

The nearest town was Latigo, where Sheriff Ross Lynch had his office. The fat rider was Gene Bates, but nothing more was said about Wat Bell or what made the sheriff so sure he could find him that he started out on a rainy day. Knowing the uncertainties of travel in the West, and the liking of sheriffs for swivel chairs, I had a hunch that somebody had tipped off the sheriff. It was less than reasonable to suppose he would start out with two men in bad weather merely on the chance that the man he sought was coming to Arizona.

Lynch looked up suddenly. "We'll be ridin' on into Latigo," he said, "and I reckon you'd better come along."

"Are you arresting me?"

His blue eyes turned mean again. He didn't like me even a

little bit. “Not necessarily,” he said, “but we’ll be wantin’ to ask you questions, and we’ll be gettin’ answers.”

“Look, my friend.” I leaned forward just a little, and having my hands on my hips as I did, the move put my gun butts practically in my palms. “I’m not planning to get stuck for something somebody else did. You rode down here and for some reason assumed I was the guilty man. Anyway, you’re all set on taking me in.

“You made no effort, and I’ll leave it to Dolliver here to check my story. You’ve sat here while the rain washed or partly washed those tracks away. You made no effort to get after those killers.

“You claim you’re hunting some killer named Wat Bell, yet when you got here, all the ambition seemed to leave you. Mister Sheriff, I’m not your man. I didn’t kill Simon Ludlow. I never saw him before. I have all the money I need and a better horse than any of you ride. Ludlow had nothing at all that I could want. The only shot I’ve fired was from my rifle, and Ludlow was shot with a pistol, and that last one was fairly close up.”

Lynch looked ugly. “I know what I’m doin’!” he stated flatly. “I’ve got my reasons!”

This looked like a good time to let them in on something. How anxious they were for gunplay, I didn’t know. I did know that I stood a much better chance right here than on the trail. I’d a sudden hunch that might be haywire as could be, but it might be correct. I’d a hunch Lynch had been told Wat Bell was coming right to the Tin Cup. I’d a further hunch that Wat Bell was not supposed to leave this ranch alive, and also that while Lynch now had doubts that I was Wat Bell, he was very apt to gun me down once I was on the road with the three of them.

“All right,” I said. “You’ve got your reasons. Well, I have mine for not going into Latigo with you! I don’t wear two guns just for fun, and if those two shots had been fired at Ludlow by me, he'd never have come back to this ranch. If you want to call my bluff and see whether I savvy guns or not, just buy chips in my game, and you'll see!"

He was madder right then than a wildcat in a swarm of bees, but he wasn't very happy about the spot he *was* in. Ross Lynch was not yellow, not by a jugful, but I knew there were several things about this setup he didn't like. The presence of Win Dolliver, who I now knew had joined him by accident, was one of them. Another was the fact that I said I was the Papago Kid. That name meant nothing to him. But if, as I now believed, he had been tipped off that Wat Bell was coming to this ranch, then I had confused the issue enough so that he wasn't sure who I was.

Also, he was no fool. He had seen those two guns, and the guns had seen use. If we cut our dogs loose in this cabin, somebody was going to get hurt besides me. Nobody knew that better than Lynch.

Dolliver smoothed things over. He was a smart hombre, that one. "There's something to what he says, Ross. After all, why should we suspect him? It could just as easily have been me who found Ludlow. I was headed this way when I met you boys.

"We should have looked for those tracks, too. I'm honest to say that I never thought of it." He turned to me. "Did you hit the man you shot at?"

"Burned him, I think. His horse was moving. I held my fire, but it was the best chance I had." Right then I decided to say nothing about the gun the rider had dropped but to have a look the first chance I got. That gun might be a clue that would help me ferret out the answer to this deal.

Lynch was getting ready to say something, and I was sure I wouldn't like it. Dolliver interrupted. "Look, Ross," he said quietly, "don't blame the Kid here for being on the prod. You can't blame him, riding into a deal like this. He certainly could have no reason to shoot Ludlow. Let him come on over to my place with me. I can use a hand for a few days, and when you want to see him, ride over. That will clear this situation up, and I think Papago will agree to work for me. I'll pay him top hand's wages."

"That's good for me," I agreed, "I'm not hunting trouble. I'll do all I can to find that killer, and if you want, I'll try to trail those men for you. I've ridden trails before," I added, and I pointed this one right at Lynch, "and found out right where they ended."

Lynch didn't like it, but no more than any other man did he have a stomach for gunplay in that close quarters. The presence of Win Dolliver was a big help and allowed him a chance to back out and save face.

The same questions kept coming into my mind. How had they learned Wat Bell was headed this way? Why had Hugh Taylor told me to ask for Bill Keys on the Tin Cup when it was owned by Ludlow? Who had killed the old man, and why?

Bill Keys was another puzzle. Taylor had said the man could be trusted, but he didn't size up right to me. How good a description did he have of me? Or did he have one at all? Hugh might not have known him so well and could have been mistaken in trusting him. For one, I was doing no talking until I understood the lay of the land.

Something else had come into my mind that somehow I'd never thought of before. When Hugh Taylor had met me that night and told me of my uncle's murder, and that I was wanted for it, I had thought of little else. True, I had left town rather suddenly after a quarrel with old Tom Bell, but that he had been murdered on the night I left for Mexico, I'd had no idea until then. Hugh had showed me the "reward" poster but had assured me that he didn't believe me guilty. He had investigators working on the crime and advised me to go away and stay in hiding until he sent for me.

My mind was full of questions. Had my uncle left a will? And to whom had he left two hundred thousand acres of his ranch? And who *had* killed him?

Bill Keys got up and turned toward the door, and my eyes dropped to his gun, absently noting that a chip had been broken from the bone handle and the break looked recent. Sheriff Ross Lynch and Bates followed him out, and then Dolliver and I. When he rode around the corner of the house, Keys was saddling a horse with which to carry the body into town.

Once around the house, I slid from the saddle and scrambled into the rocks. A hasty look showed me only one thing: the gun was gone!

Win Dolliver looked at me curiously but said nothing until we were well along the trail to the Tumbling T. It was just six miles, and Dolliver talked pleasantly and easily of the country, the cattle, and the rain. Ludlow had been running only about six hundred head, while he had four times that many. Keys and Bates, holding a ranch in partnership, ran a few head over west.

When we were in sight of his own ranch, Win turned. "Did you get a good look at those riders? Enough to know them again?"

"No," I admitted, realizing this was the first pointed question he had asked and wondering what was behind it, "but one of them lost a gun back there. When I looked ... it was gone."

"Maybe you just didn't find it?"

"No, I saw where it had been. There was a boot track near it."

We didn't say anything more right then, because the door opened and a girl stepped out on the porch, and I forgot everything I had been thinking and all that had happened.

There is no description for a girl like that. It was simply that this was the girl I had been looking for all my life. It wasn't a matter of eyes nor hair, although hers were beautiful, it was simply that here she was, the girl that was meant for me. She was trimly shaped and neat, and there was quick laughter in her eyes, and there was interest and appraisal, too.

"Mag," Dolliver said, swinging down, "meet the Papago Kid. He's riding through the country and has had a little trouble with Ross Lynch."

"That's nothing against him on the T!" Maggie Dolliver replied with spirit. "You know what I think of Ross."

Win chuckled. "Everybody should after the way you told him off at the last Latigo dance. But what about Howie Taber?"

She flushed, and I didn't miss that. The name struck me, too.

"Who did you say?" I asked.

"Taber. He is a partner of Lynch's in a ranch they have out here. At least, Taber owns the ranch, and Lynch runs the cows when he's not working at being sheriff. Pretty well off, Taber is. And he made quite a play for Maggie when he was out here last."

* * * * *

Maggie made better coffee than Win, I found, and her cookies were wonderful. I listened, mostly, and answered a few random questions about Mexico. Then I started in and asked my first question.

"What about Keys? Who is he?"

"Keys?" The question puzzled Dolliver. "Frankly, I don't like the man. He ranches some with Bates, as I said, and he and Lynch are thicker than thieves. There's a story around that he ran with that horse-stealing outfit down in the Bradshaws, but I wouldn't know how true it is. He's also supposed to be something of a gun hawk. He has killed one man I know of . . . a drifter in Latigo."

Maggie looked at me curiously, then a thought seemed to occur to her, and she turned to Win. "What I can't understand is why anyone would want to kill a nice old man like Simon Ludlow."

"It was a mistake," I said, repeating what I had overheard when I rode up on the killers. "I think they were looking for someone else."

"But who?" Win puzzled. "And why?"

"I think," I said deliberately, "they were looking for me. I think they saw a rider at the expected place and shot him, then finished him off to prevent him talking when they found their mistake."

"But who was it they were after?" Maggie demanded.

"Me," I repeated dryly. "I think they wanted me."

Moreover, I told myself, if they had wished to kill me and had failed, they would surely try again. Had they been sure that I was Wat Bell rather than the Papago Kid, they would have insisted I go to town with them and shot me, "trying to escape" on the way in. As it was, probably Win Dolliver's presence had saved me at first sight.

"Don't take what I said about working too seriously," Win volunteered, after a moment. "My main idea was to get you away from Lynch without a fight. He's tough, and he didn't like you. I could see that. Dangerous as he is, I think you've more to fear from Bill Keys."

Neither of them asked me any questions, nor why I believed it had been me the killers wanted. Whatever their reason for inviting me here, and I was convinced there was a reason, they asked no questions and offered no information.

III

Nevertheless, I was up at daybreak with the hands, ate breakfast with them and with Win, and rode out to work with them. Later in the morning, when Maggie came out to join us, I overheard him tell her: "Whatever else he may be, Mag, he's a hand. He's done more work than any two of the regular boys."

Maybe it was because these cedar brakes were easy after brush-popping down in the Big Bend, where I had worked two years, but I did get a lot done. And maybe because it was good to have a rope in my hands and a cow by the tail instead of only a gun. Yet all the time I worked, my mind was busy, and it didn't like what seemed to be the truth.

A lot of loose ends were beginning to find their way to a common point, and I had begun to see that in skipping out of Texas, I had made a big mistake. Hugh Taylor, aside from being my cousin was also my friend, or so I had believed. From anyone but him, I would never have taken the advice he had given.

Hugh Taylor had run off from the ranch where we were growing up when he was sixteen, and returned again after four years. After being around a year, he took off again, and returned some months later with money and a silver-mounted saddle. He was bigger than I and rugged. He was also two years older. A top hand at anything he did, he stood high in my uncle's favor.

Yet I'd worked on at the ranch, never leaving, punching cows, mending fence, riding herd. I had taken two herds north over the trail, and I'd had a gunfight in Abilene and killed my man. I wasn't proud of that, and as only a few of the trail hands returned, and they promised not to talk, nobody around the XY knew. Later, when I was down in the Big Bend with a bunch of cattle, we had trouble with Mexican bandits, and I went into their camp, brought back some stolen horses, and did it without firing a shot.

Finally, when I was twenty-four, Uncle Tom and I had a big argument, and I got mad and lit out for Mexico. Crossing the border, I didn't want to be known as Uncle Tom Bell's nephew, so I called myself the Papago Kid. Riding through Coahuila to Durango, I had several fights, and then moving up into Sonora, I tied up with old Valverdes and protected his ranch against bandits. While there I had two more gunfights, one with a Mexican gunman, the other with an American.

Then, after being away two years, I had returned across the border, and the first person I'd met was Hugh. At the time it seemed a stroke of luck, and I remember how startled he was to see me.

"You here, Wat?" he had exclaimed. "Don't you know you're wanted for murder?"

That got me, and in reply to my heated questions, he told me that the night after our quarrel, Uncle Tom had been shot and killed, that I was sought as the killer, but a story had returned to the XY that I had been killed by bandits in Mexico.

"Your best bet is to get out of here," he told me. "Ride west to Arizona. I've some friends out there, and in the meantime I'll do what I can to straighten this up."

So my uncle was dead, and they believed I had killed him. I hadn't, but somebody else had, and who was that somebody? Also, what kind of a deal had Hugh sent me into at the Tin Cup? I arrive to find a man murdered, and the sheriff hunting a Texas outlaw known as Wat Bell—and knowing exactly where to find him and when.

That last didn't make sense until I began to remember my last stop before getting there. It had been in Lincoln, New Mexico, and I had stopped there with a friend of Hugh Taylor's. Now if that friend had wired Sheriff Lynch, and Lynch had done a little figuring as to miles a day, it would not be too hard to arrive at the day of my arrival at the Tin Cup—a sufficiently secluded spot for murder.

Uncle Tom Bell had no relatives anyone knew of but Hugh and myself, so he would naturally leave his two hundred thousand acres to us, and if one of us died, then the other would inherit everything. I didn't like to think that of Hugh, but he had been a little greedy, I remembered, even as a youngster.

A few discreet inquiries around proved that nobody had ever heard of Hugh Taylor, yet Taylor knew people here, and they knew him. I was still studying about that when Mag loped her pony over to where I sat my horse watching the herd we'd bunched.

"Win tells me you're a hand," she said, smiling at me. "I hope you decide to stay. He likes you, and it will be lonesome for him after I leave."

That hit me hard. I turned in my saddle. "After you leave? Then you're going away?"

She must have seen something in my face, because hers suddenly changed, and the smile went out of it. "I … I'm going to be married," she said quietly.

That was all. Neither of us had another thing to say right

then. For me, she had said it all. If in all the world there was a girl for me, this was the one. I wanted her as I never had wanted anything. But I was just the Papago Kid and a fugitive from the law.

What she was thinking, I have no idea, but she didn't look happy. We just sat there watching the herd until it started to move. There were enough men to handle it, and I made no move to follow.

"You're quiet," she said finally, "you don't say anything."

"What can I say?" I asked her honestly enough. "You've just said it all."

She didn't act mystified and want an explanation, for she knew as well as I what I meant and how I felt. She did finally say something, and it was so much what a lot of girls would have said that it enabled me to get my feet on the ground again.

She said: "You've only known me a few hours."

"How long does it take? Is there a special time, or something? A special set of rules that says flatly a man has to know a girl three weeks, seventeen hours, and nine minutes before he can fall in love with her? And another set that says she must know him six months, four hours, and five minutes before she can admit she likes him?

"There isn't any time limit and there never has been," I told her. "To some people it comes quick, to others slow. With me it was the minute you walked out on the porch back there, and I rode into the yard. That's exactly when it was. The rest doesn't matter."

My voice wasn't a lover's voice. It was pretty sharp and hard, because I felt just that way. Then it hit me all of a sudden, and I could see it plain as day.

"Well, at least he didn't steal you!"

She looked up quickly, her eyes going wide with surprise. "Steal me? Who?"

"Hugh Taylor," I said.

"Who?" she looked puzzled and a little frightened. "What do you mean?"

"I mean Howie Taber … the one who was a friend of Lynch's, only his name is Hugh Taylor, and he's my cousin."

"Your cousin?" She was staring at me now, but there was not so much surprise in her eyes as I had expected. "What are you talking about?"

"I'm talking about a big, blond, and handsome man with broad shoulders and deep-set blue eyes, a man with a small scar on the point of his chin, who rides good horses and wears flashy clothes and handles a gun well. That's who I mean. A man who is my cousin but who could easily have called himself Howie Taber."

Her face was white now, but she was staring right through me. "And what is your name?" she demanded.

"I'm Wat Bell," I told her. "I am the man Lynch was looking for at the Tin Cup, and how did he know I'd be there? Only one man in all the world knew it, and that man was Hugh … who I thought was my best friend."

"I don't believe that," she said, "I don't believe any of it. You may know him, but you're an outlaw, masquerading under a false name. You've made all this up."

"All right," I said, "I made it up." With that I reined my horse around and started back for the T. If I had been riding Rowdy, I'd never have gone back at all, but this was a cow horse I'd borrowed, wanting to save the big black after his long trek across country.

There was only one thing in my mind then, to get Rowdy and hit the trail out of there, but fast. And where to? Back to Texas! To prove that I hadn't killed my uncle. To prove that I was no outlaw.

The cow horse I was on was a good horse, and he took me

over the hill to the T at a fast lope, and I came up from behind the corrals and hit the dirt and then stopped. Right there across the yard from me was Ross Lynch, and beside him was Gene Bates. Win Dolliver was on the step, and his face looked dark as death and just as solemn.

Lynch stepped out toward me and stopped. "Wat Bell!" he said. "I arrest you for murder!"

"Whose murder?" I demanded.

"The murder of Simon Ludlow!" he said. Then he smiled. "There is a charge against you in Texas, but we'll hang you for this one!"

I was mad all the way through. My hands swinging at my sides, I looked at him. "Ross Lynch, I did not murder Ludlow, and you damned well know it. You know it because you know who did. And I know. It was …"

Gene Bates's hand swept down for a gun, as did the hand of Lynch. My own guns were coming up, and I took a quick step forward and right and fired quickly—too quickly. My first bullet knocked the gun from the sheriff's hand, and I hadn't intended it that way. I wanted to kill him. The second one took Gene Bates right over the belt buckle.

Win Dolliver hadn't moved. He stood there on the steps, his eyes wide. But what he thought, he wasn't saying. I don't know where Maggie was. On the bunkhouse steps were two of the boys, and another one stood at the corral. He turned to his saddle pockets and dug out a box of .44s.

"Catch!" he said simply, and tossed it.

"Thanks!" I caught the box in my left hand and backed toward the corral.

Lynch was holding his numbed hand and staring at me.

"I'll kill you for this!" he said. "I'll kill you if it's the last thing I do!"

"If you do, it will be," I told him.

Astride the cow pony, I looked at Win. "Thanks, Dolliver. You've been mighty square. Simon Ludlow was killed by Gene Bates and Bill Keys. That chip on the bone handle of Keys's gun was broken off when it fell into the rocks, you know where."

Then I reined my horse around and hit the trail at a fast run.

* * * * *

That pony had worked hard, but he was game. He stayed with that run until he hit timber, and then I slowed him down to a canter and then to a walk. After that, I began to Injun my trail. I took so many twists and turns, I was dizzy, and I rode up and down several streams, across several shelves of rock, and through some sand. And then I doubled back and headed for the Tin Cup.

My horse wouldn't go far, and he needed rest. I needed food. There was food in the cabin, and every chance they wouldn't think of it right away. Also, it was within striking distance of the T, and I had no idea of leaving Rowdy. That big black horse meant a lot to me, and ever since old Valverdes gave him to me, I'd treated him like a child.

Now I was an outlaw, having resisted arrest, the first crime I'd committed. But if I could prove that Bates and Keys had killed Ludlow, and with the sheriff's knowledge, I'd be in the clear even on that. And it was something I intended to prove.

From the expression on Lynch's face, I knew that shooting of mine had been a distinct shock. Hugh hadn't warned them about that simply because he didn't know. Hugh had always beaten me in shooting matches. That was before I went to Mexico. He had probably told Lynch I was only a fair shot. Well, the shooting that knocked the gun from his hand and drilled Bates had been good shooting, the kind he wouldn't be too anxious to tackle again.

By sundown I was bedded down in the pines, watching the Tin Cup ranch house. All through the final hours of daylight, I watched it and studied the trails. I wanted no traps laid for me, although I doubted if they would think of the Tin Cup right away.

* * * * *

It was well after midnight before I started down the trail to the ranch, and I took my horse only a short distance, then left him tied in the brush and cat-footed it down by myself, leaving my spurs on the horn of my saddle.

Nothing looked very good right then. I had killed Gene Bates and resisted arrest. Hugh Taylor, who I'd considered my best friend, had tried to trap me into an ambush, and Maggie Dolliver, the girl I wanted more than anything in life, was in love with Hugh. Right then I'd about as little to live for as any man, but I'd a lot of resentment—nor was I one to bow my head before the storm and ride off letting well enough alone.

When I did ride off, it would be with my name clear, and also I would know and the world would know who had killed Uncle Tom Bell. Until then, I had a job to do.

The warm sun of the late afternoon had baked the ground hard after the rain, and I moved carefully. The stone house was dark and still when I tried the door, and it eased open without a sound. Once inside I wasted no time, for while Win had been making coffee on the day of the killing, I had seen where the food was kept. Hastily, I reached for the coffee sack. It was almost empty!

Puzzled, for it had been nearly full when 1 last saw it, I

reached for the beans, and they were gone. And then there was a whisper of movement behind me, and I turned, palming my gun as I moved.

"Don't shoot!" The voice was low, but the very sound of it thrilled me so that I couldn't have squeezed a trigger if I'd wished. "The food is on the table, all packed."

"Mag! You did this for me?"

I couldn't believe that, and moved around the table toward her. She had been in that inner room, waiting behind the blanket covered door.

"Yes." The word was simple and honest. "I did it for you, and I've no idea whether I'm doing right or not. Maybe all they say about you is true. Maybe you did kill your uncle, and maybe you did kill Simon Ludlow."

"You don't believe that?"

"No," she hesitated, "no, I don't believe I do. I know Ross Lynch, Wat … that's your name, isn't it? He has been mixed up in so many wrong things. It was the only fault I could find with Howie … that he trailed with Lynch and that devil, Bill Keys."

In the darkness I could not see her eyes, but suddenly my hands lifted to her shoulders. "Mag," I said softly, "I've got to ride out of here. Whatever else I do, I've got to clear myself, and I'm going to do it, and if the trouble strays over on somebody else's range, I'm going to follow it there.

"I could go away now, taking the blame for Ludlow like they've already hung the blame on me for Uncle Tom, but I won't do it. I won't have you doubting me, even if I never see you again. Nor do I want folks to think I've killed Uncle Tom, after he did so much for me."

She didn't say anything for a moment, and with her arms all warm under my hands, it was all I could do to keep from drawing her close. Finally, she spoke.

"Do what you have to do, Wat. I know how you feel."

"But, Mag, suppose that somebody you ... well, I mean, suppose that when I find who did this killing, I find it was somebody close to you. What then?"

She looked up at me again. "Why, then, Wat, it would have to be that way. I guess I knew you felt like this, I knew who you believed was guilty, but I came here and got this food ready for you, sure that you'd come. I brought your horse, too, Wat. He's in the shadow by the stable."

"Rowdy?" My voice lifted, then lowered. "You did that? Oh, you darling! Now I'll feel like a man again. This pony, he tries hard, and he's got a great heart, but he's not Rowdy."

"I knew how you felt about him." She drew back. "Now you'd better go. Ride out of here, and good luck, whatever you do, or whatever comes!"

IV

That was just the way I left, with that pack over my shoulder, slipping out to find Rowdy, who nudged me with his nose and stamped contentedly. But I waited there until she was on her horse and gone, and then I slid into the saddle and headed for the hills. When I got to where I'd left the pony, I tied the bridle reins up and turned him loose, knowing he'd find his way back to the T.

Already I'd had an idea. Bill Keys had come from the Bradshaws, and that was where I was heading, right for Horsethief Canyon. There had to be a tie-up there. Nor was I waiting until morning. Rowdy was rested and ready for the trail, and I took it, riding west across the mountains, skirting Latigo, and heading on west. On the third night, I camped at Badger Spring, up a creek from the canyon of the Agua Fria, and, after a quick breakfast in the morning, crossed the Bumblebee and Black Canyon and headed up the Dead Cow. Skirting the peak on a bench, I cut down the mountainside into Horsethief Canyon.

Western men knew the West, and it was no wonder that even as far east as Dimmit County, Texas, we knew about the horse thief trails that cut through the country from Robber's Roost and the Hole in the Wall to Mexico. This place was only a way station, but, from all I'd heard, I knew some of the crowd that trailed stolen horses, and they were a hard bunch of men.

Rowdy had a feeling for trouble. The big black pricked his ears toward the ramshackle cluster of cabins and corrals that lay on the flat among the mountains. Nobody needed to tell me that we were watched all the way down that trail, and when Rowdy drew up in front of the combination saloon and store that was the headquarters at Horsethief, a half-dozen men idled on the steps.

Across at the big barn, a man sat on a bench with a Henry rifle across his knees, and another man whittled idly in front of a cabin even further along.

When I swung down, I tied Rowdy to the rail and stepped up on the porch and dug out the makings.

"Howdy," I offered.

A lean, hatchet-faced man who looked the type to murder his mother-in-law, looked up.

"Howdy."

Nobody said anything, and when I'd built a smoke, I offered the tobacco around, but nobody made a move to accept. A short, stocky rider with run-down heels on his boots squatted against the wall. He looked up at me, then nodded at Rowdy.

"Quite a hoss. Looks like he could make miles."

"He made 'em to here." I looked at Shorty again. "Want a drink? I'll buy."

He got up with alacrity. "Never refused a drink!" he warned me.

We pushed through the doors and bellied up to the bar. There was a smell of cured bacon, dry goods, and spices curiously intermingled. I glanced around the store and sized up the fat man in the dirty shirt who bounced around to the bar side and made a casual swipe at the bar top with a rag.

"What'll it be, gents?"

Shorty chuckled. "He says 'what'll it be' ever'time, and he ain't had nothing but Injun whiskey over this bar in a year!"

Fatty was indignant. "Injun whiskey, my eye!" he exploded. "This here's my own make, and mighty good rye likker, if I do say so! Injun whiskey!" he snorted. "You've been drinkin' out of horse tracks and buffalo wallers so long, you don't know a good drink when you get one!" He placed two glasses on the bar and a bottle.

Shorty poured for them both, but Fatty reached for the bottle as he put it down.

"Leave the bottle," I told him, "we'll want another." I placed a gold piece on the bar, and Fatty picked it up so fast, it looked like a wink of light.

"Better not flash that coin around if you've got more of it," Shorty warned. "Especially when Wolf Kettle is around. He's the hombre you talked to out yonder, and while Davis is away, he's ramroddin' the outfit."

"Things look kind of slow," I suggested.

"They sure are!" Shorty's disgust was evident. "Nothing doing at all! From what we hear, there's to be something big movin' soon, but you can't tell. Where you from?"

"Down Sonora way. They call me the Papago Kid."

"Shorty Carver's my handle." He looked up at me. "Sonora, is it? Well, I sure figured I knew you." He spoke softly all of a sudden. "I'd've sworn you were an hombre I saw sling a gun up to Dodge, one time. An hombre name of Wat Bell, from a Texas outfit."

"If you think I look like him," I suggested, "forget it. He might not like the resemblance!"

Shorty laughed. "Sure thing! You can be anybody you want with me. What's on your mind? You wantin' to join up?"

"Not exactly. I'm huntin' a couple of friends of mine. Bill Keys and an hombre named Taber."

Shorty Carver's face hardened. "You won't find 'em here, and if they are friends of yours, sure you'd better hunt another sidekick than me. That Taber and I didn't get along."

I took a sidelong look at Shorty. "He's been here then?"

"Been here?" Shorty looked around at me. "He was here yesterday!"

"What?"

My question was so sharp that a half dozen heads turned our way, and I lowered my voice.

"Did you say … yesterday?"

"Sure did! He rode in here about suppertime, and him and Davis had a long confab. Then Davis takes off for Skull Valley, and where Taber went, I don't know. He rode out of here, headin' east."

For several minutes I didn't say a word. If Hugh was out here, that meant the time for a showdown had come. Yet what had I found? Nothing to date that would help. That Hugh Taylor had been known to the outlaws of Horsethief Canyon was something, but not much.

Right then I began to wonder for the first time about those absences from the ranch when Hugh was growing up. And that time he had returned with that silver mounted saddle and a good bit of money. It was becoming more apparent where that money had come from. Had Uncle Tom Bell guessed? He was a sharp old man and had not ridden the trails and plains for nothing. He could read sign wherever it was … and here was another thought: perhaps he had read the truth and guessed at what lay behind those absences and jumped Hugh about it.

Had Hugh killed his uncle?

There was enough of the old feeling for Hugh left to make me revolt at the idea, and yet it began to seem more and more possible. Uncle Tom and I had had a violent quarrel, and I left. What would be easier than to kill him and let me take the blame? His surprise at my sudden return could have come from his consternation at what it might mean to him, and also he might have believed those rumors that I had been killed in Mexico.

Certainly, he managed to get me out of the country without seeing anyone else.

The swinging doors shoved wide, and Kettle came in. He took a sidelong glance at me and walked up to the bar at my side and ordered a drink. I could smell trouble coming and could see there was something in Kettle's craw.

He got his drink and turned to me. "We don't welcome strangers here!" he said. "State your business, and ride on out!"

That turned me around, but I took my time. The man irritated me, and I didn't feel like sidestepping trouble. I was tired of running and ready for a showdown, and ready to back it with lead.

"Kettle," I said clearly, "I didn't come in here to see you. I never heard of you. You may run a big herd where you come from, but where I ride that herd looks like a mighty small gathering!"

His face darkened a little, and the yellow lights in his eyes were plainer. He half turned before I spoke, but I gave it to him fast.

"Don't try to run any blazers on me, Kettle, because they won't stick. If you make rough talk with me, it's gun talk, and if you draw on me, I'll kill you!"

Shorty Carver had stepped wide of me and was standing there facing the room. What his play would be, I couldn't know. He was a friend of only a few minutes, yet there had been some spark of comradeship there, such as one often finds with men of the same ilk and the same background. He spoke before either of us could make a move.

"He came to see Taber and Keys," Shorty warned. "They sent for him!"

"What?" Carver's statement obviously stopped Kettle. "How do you know that?"

"Because I told him," I said simply.

He glared at me suspiciously. Something was gnawing at the man, and it might be something about me, but I had the feeling that he was naturally mean, a trouble hunter, a man with a burr under his saddle.

"Where'd you know Taber?" he demanded.

"In Texas," I said calmly, "and I knew Bill Keys in Sonora." That last was sheer hope, for whether Keys had ever been below the border, I didn't know.

"He's the Papago Kid," Carver said.

"Never heard of him!" Kettle returned sharply.

Another man spoke up, a lean-faced man with a drooping black mustache. "I have," he said. "He's the hombre that killed Albie Dick."

Kettle's eyes sharpened, and I knew that meant something to this man. Albie Dick had been a dangerous man, and a killer with fifteen dead men on his trail when we tangled in Sonora.

"That's neither here nor there," I said calmly. "I want to talk to Howie Taber."

"You'll have to wait," Kettle said grudgingly. "He ain't here."

Somehow, men relaxed. Shorty returned to the bar and took another drink. "You'd better watch yourself," he warned under his breath. "Wolf was never braced like that before. He'll be careful to make his play at the right time, but you've got trouble. The man's mean as a rattler."

He downed his drink. "Also," he added, "I'm beginning to remember things. That Wat Bell who downed that man in Abilene was ramrodding an XY herd … and that's the ranch we're going to use in Texas!"

"What do you mean? Going to use?"

He looked at me quickly, sharply. "So? You don't know the inside on this, do you?" He was silent, tracing circles on the bar with the bottom of his glass. "Just what is between you and Taber, Kid?"

That was a sticker, and I hesitated. Shorty had said earlier that he had no use for Taber. Right then I knew my time here was short, and a friend would be a help. Another enemy would be little worse.

"Taber's my cousin," I said frankly, speaking low. "I think he killed my uncle and framed me with the murder while I was in Mexico. Furthermore, I think he sent me out here to lay low and planned to have me murdered when I arrived."

Quietly, I explained in as few words as possible, and from time to time he nodded.

"Glad you told me," he said. "Also, there's no posters on Wat Bell out here, so you must be right on figuring that Lynch was out to get you."

"No posters on me? How do you know that?"

He grinned, and he said softly: "Because I'm a Cattle Associ-ation detective, pardner, and I'm studyin' into the biggest steal of horses and cattle ever organized."

Together we walked outside, and the story he told me answered a lot of questions. For several years a steady stream of stolen stock had been sent south over the old horse thief trail from the Hole in the Wall and Robber's Roost to Mexico, and this valley was one of the important way stations. Lately, it had become apparent that even larger things were in the wind, for a man lately associated with the gang had suddenly become owner of a Panhandle Ranch in Texas. There was a reported tie-up with the XY in central southern Texas, and large quantities of stock had begun to disappear and move south toward the border. It had begun to look as if mass stealings of stock had begun, moving south under cover and with large ranches as way stations.

"Who's behind it?" I asked him. "Any guesses on that?"

"Uhn-huh. There is." Shorty Carver lit a smoke. "Howie Taber's behind it. That cousin of yours has turned out to be the brains of the biggest stock-stealing ring in the country."

From the time he was sixteen until he was twenty, Hugh Taylor had been absent from the XY. He had gone again shortly after, and obviously he had been gone at least once during the time I was in Mexico. It was then, no doubt, that he had begun to round up old cronies of his earlier days and build the ring that Carver now told me about.

"Shorty," I said, "can you slip out of here?"

"Uhn-huh."

"Then wire the sheriff in Dimmit County. See if I'm really wanted there for murder. Also, check on Tom Bell's will, see who that XY spread was left to when he died. I'm having a talk with that cousin of mine." I hesitated, thinking. "See you at the Tin Cup."

"Watch your step!" Shorty warned. "Hugh isn't so bad, but you watch Bill Keys and Kettle."

V

After he was gone, I idled around, getting the lay of the land and thinking things over. It was well along in the afternoon, and night soon to come. By this time Hugh would know that I was still alive, that the plot to get me at the Tin Cup had failed.

Evidently, the Tin Cup had been chosen because of its secluded position, and that Lynch and Keys had been informed by the friend where I had stopped last that I was coming. Accordingly, they had evidently waited. It might be that I had been spotted and reported at several places since then, and they had come out to meet me, either at the Tin Cup or on the trail near there.

Probably they had managed to get Ludlow away from his ranch, or had reason to believe he would be away. Then they had either killed him by mistake, or had killed him because he returned too soon. No doubt they had plans for the Tin Cup, anyway, as the ranch was ideal for such a venture as they planned.

The jumpiness was in me now that presaged danger. I could sense it all around me, and I was restless. Every man here would be an enemy once it was realized who I was, and at any moment

Bill Keys, Hugh Taylor, or Ross Lynch might ride in, and then the lid would blow off. I was surrounded by unfriendly guns, and to blast my way out would be a forlorn hope.

Mingled with the realization of my danger was an acute longing to be back with Maggie Dolliver. No woman had ever affected me as she had, and despite the fact that there was an understanding between herself and Hugh, I had the feeling that she had felt for me as I had for her. That she had brought Rowdy to me and packed the food was enough to show that she believed in me.

Time and again I walked down to the corral to talk to Rowdy. Time and again I noted exactly where my saddle was and calculated every move it would take to re-saddle him. That was something I wanted to do, but not until it was dark. To saddle him now would serve only as a warning of impending departure. I wanted them to believe that I was content to await the return of the man they knew as Howie Taber.

Yet I could feel the suspicion, and my own restlessness contributed to it. Wolf watched me sharply, his yellowish eyes rarely leaving me. Other men seemed always around, but apparently Shorty Carver had managed to slip away. Being accepted here, his going and coming would occasion little remark.

My thoughts kept reverting to Maggie and Win. At least Win was my friend, and it was something to have even one friend now.

Once more I returned to the saloon and seated myself in a chair against the wall, careful to keep my guns clear. Evening was coming, and the sun had slipped down behind Wasson Peak and the ridges around it. All the bright glare of the Arizona sun was gone, and the desert and mountains had turned to soft pastel shades. A blue quail called out in the brush, and somewhere a burro yawned his lonely call into the cool air of twilight. A door slammed, and then I heard water splashing as someone dipped a bucket into the spring. There was a subdued murmur of voices, and the rattle of dishes. There was no hunger in me, only that poised alertness that kept my eyes moving and my every muscle and nerve aware and ready.

Casually, I arose to my feet and stretched. Then as I had a dozen times before, I sauntered carelessly down to the corral. Wolf Kettle watched me, but I ignored him, stopping near the corrals to look around, then I stepped over and put my hand on Rowdy's neck and spoke to him. After a minute I crawled through the poles and was out of sight of Wolf or any of the others.

My movements were swift and sure. Rowdy was never bridled or saddled faster in his life, and in what seemed scarcely no time, I was sauntering back into sight, crawling once more through the corral bar. I slowly rolled a smoke, struck a match, and then ambled placidly and nonchalantly back toward the store.

"Brother," I told myself, "if you get out of here with a whole skin, you're lucky."

Back in my chair, I listened to the casual talk, scarcely paying attention until suddenly two horses rounded into sight. They were walking, and they came so suddenly that it was a surprise to all of us. They came from the other side of the saloon and stopped at the end of the porch opposite me.

Two men swung down.

"Wolf? You got some grub ready?"

It was Hugh Taylor!

My heart pounding, I slowly lowered my hands to my knees, my eyes riveted on him.

"You'd better have." The second man was speaking, and it was Bill Keys. "I'm hungry as a grizzly!"

It was late dusk, and no faces could be distinguished. Hugh came up on the porch, looking tall, strong, and familiar. Suddenly, it was hard to think of him as being an outlaw, an enemy. I could only recall the times we went swimming together, the horses we swapped, and the times we played hooky from school and went hunting.

He happened to turn his head then, and he looked right at me. He could have seen no more than a black figure of a man, seated there, but there must have been something familiar about it.

"Who's that?" His voice rang sharply.

"It's me, Hugh," I said softly. "I figured it was about time we had a little talk."

At my voice Keys jerked like he'd been struck, and he turned. Wolf was facing me, too. The three of them ringed around me, from my extreme left to full front. On the right side, the edge of the porch, there was no one.

"You … Wat?"

There was an edge of something in his voice, doubt, unc-er-tainty, or something. Maybe he was remembering, too.

"We've nothing to talk about, nothing at all," he said.

"What about Uncle Tom, Hugh? I didn't kill him … Did you?"

His breath drew sharply. "We won't talk about that, Wat. Not right now. You shouldn't have come here, you know that."

"Do I, Hugh? You sent me to the Tin Cup, didn't you? Was I supposed to be killed there? Did you figure to send your own cousin, who grew up with you, to get killed?"

I knew Western men. Even the outlaws were rarely cruel men. Many of them were cowpunchers who had rustled the wrong stock once too often, some of them were men who had been too handy with a gun, but few of them were really bad men. Rather they were often reckless and careless in a land where many men were reckless and where property rights were uncertain. Among them were, of course, killers and men of criminal instincts, yet I was playing for those others.

He didn't answer me, so I went on talking, not raising my voice, just an easy conversational tone, yet all the time every nerve was on edge.

"They killed the wrong man, Hugh, and now I'm looking into things. I've been asking questions … about Uncle Tom's will and whether I'm really wanted for murder or not, and now I'm getting mighty curious about you."

"You're too curious." His mind seemed to be made up, and I sensed an almost regretful note. "You should never have come back from Mexico, Wat. You messed up everything when you did that. You should have stayed down there. Now you're into something that's too big for you … you're playing with company that's too fast."

"Am I?" I laughed, although there was no humor in it. "No, I'm not, Hugh. You've just continued to think of me as your kid cousin. I've covered a lot of country since then, and traveled in faster company than you'll ever know."

"That's right, boss," it was the man with the black mustache again, "this hombre is the Papago Kid. He rubbed out Albie Dick and led the roundup of his outfit. Nobody got away."

"So the kid's grown up!" There was an edge of sarcasm in Hugh's voice. "That makes it a little better. I'd not like to be responsible for anybody taking advantage of you."

"You've still got a chance, Hugh," I said quietly. "You can break this up right now. Turn the killers of Ludlow over to the law, confess your part in this plot, and leave the country."

"Are you crazy?" He was genuinely angry now. "You! Giving *me* a chance!"

"Then your answer is no?"

I could see that Bill Keys and Kettle were growing restive. For their taste we had talked too long, and neither of them liked the tone of it.

"You fool!" Contempt was thick in his voice. "You should never have come back from Mexico! Worse, you should have never come here! You should have hightailed it out of the country! I don't want to kill you, but there's no choice!"

There was one more thing. Nor could I resist it.

"How could I leave, Hugh? I fell in love with Maggie."

"What?" He wheeled so quickly to face toward me again that he gave me the one big break I'd needed. I went off that porch in one jump and ducked around the corner of the house. I'd never have dared chance it with Keys and Kettle having their eyes on me, but when Hugh turned, he partially blocked them off. I hit the ground running and skidded into the shadow of a clump of mesquite. Then I gave out with a piercing whistle.

One shot cut the brush in reply to my whistle, but that whistle stopped them. They didn't know what it meant. It seemed like a signal, and they were immediately afraid I had help nearby. It was a signal, but not for help. It was for Rowdy.

He knew what to do. On that signal he would untie himself if tied with a slip knot, or nose down corral bars. It was a trick I'd taught him, along with a dozen others.

The rattle of hoofs sounded, and I heard somebody yell. "The corral's open! Somebody's there!"

I whistled again, and the big black horse wheeled between the buildings. Somebody cracked down on me again, and that time I had enough of being the target in a shooting gallery. I glimpsed a dark form and let fly, and heard a grunt and the sound of something falling, and then I was in the saddle and taking off across the valley.

My route was in my mind. I'd gotten it from Shorty, who knew the area.

Rowdy took off down Horsethief Canyon at a dead run, then slowed and turned sharply left up a trail to the bench. We had the mountain for a background and were lost in the blackness there, and Rowdy could walk like a cat when the chips were down. We crossed the shoulder of the mountain south of the ranch and hit the head of Sycamore, and down Sycamore to the trail that ran south, running parallel to Black Canyon. Then I crossed the table to the Agua Fria again, and took off up Squaw Creek.

The advantage of darkness and the best horse was mine, and I used it. Danger would come with morning, but I was hoping that Shorty would meet me at the Tumbling T with news that was good. Whatever else happened, I would see Maggie once more, and it was worth the ride and worth the danger.

* * * * *

Morning lifted the darkness away and brought back the sun-bright hills to view. I liked the feel of the country and the air on my face, and the feel of a good horse between my knees. Behind me was the end of something, the end of all the old days when I was a kid on the XY, of Uncle Tom Bell, crabby and lovable, but honest as the day—and Hugh, older than I and skillful in all things. We'd never been close, and yet we'd done a lot together as boys will, and we had grown older together. It is a sad thing to leave a friend behind, to find one you've admired changed.

When the sun was high, I turned into a deep arroyo and found a wide shadow where I could swing down and strip the saddle from Rowdy. After I'd cared for him, I picketed him on a little grass, then slept for an hour. After I'd eaten, I saddled up again. The sun had bridged the space that divides morning from afternoon and, still blazing hot, had turned just a little toward the west when I started on. Altogether I'd spent nearly three hours in the arroyo.

The sun reflected from a distant flat rock, and the clouds left shadows on the desert floor. I studied the far reach of the valley and then kept to the low ground, moving in shadows of clouds and up washes and where the ground was broken, yet I saw no one. We were headed for a showdown, Rowdy and I, but it would be at the T, or maybe the Tin Cup. It would not be here.

* * * * *

The Tin Cup lay chill and quiet in the moonlight when Rowdy walked down the trail. We drew up, looking the place over, and it was still as death. The comparison came into my mind and made me shiver a little. That was striking too close to the truth.

Skirting the place warily, I seemed to detect a darker spot among the pines, and circled toward it. Then I drew up and listened. I heard a horse stamp and blow, then stillness. Speaking to Rowdy so he would not whinny, I moved in.

A lone man was camped in the pines near a stream. Watching it, I heard a light footfall, then turned. Shorty Carver was standing there on the edge of the brush.

"Rolled my bed up and laid out in the brush myself," he said. "Figured it some safer. They might get wary of me."

He held out two wires, and shielding the flame with my hat, I struck a match and read them.

> Discharged Mexican hand confessed slaying of Bell.
> No one wanted here.

A distinct feeling of relief hit me, just as much for Hugh as for myself. If he had taken advantage of my absence to claim the ranch all for himself, I could not have blamed him, but if he had killed Uncle Tom … I ripped open the other message.

> Tom Bell's will leaves XY to Wat Bell when he returns. Bell's reason was 'he stayed with me and helped to build it.' In event of Bell's not returning, ranch to go to Hugh Taylor.

So, then I was not a fugitive but owner of two hundred thousand acres of rangeland and a huge herd of cattle. Somehow, I couldn't find it in me to blame Hugh too much. Probably he had believed me killed in Mexico, and that he was the owner of the XY. This crooked business was another thing. Uncle Tom would turn over in his grave if he thought the old XY was being used as a clearing ground or holding ground for rustled stock.

"We're heading for the T," I told Carver. "You've seen these messages?"

"Read 'em when they came in," he said. "Taylor tried to have you ambushed here. That isn't a theory any more. We've got Ross Lynch."

"Got him? Arrested?"

"Yeah, last night. There was hell to pay in Latigo. We found Ross in the hills with some rustled stock, and he ran for it. We got him in Latigo. He confessed on his deathbed."

VI

Right then I knew we were in the wrong place. If Ross Lynch had been shot down and confessed, by this time Hugh would know it—so would Keys and Kettle!

In that event they would know their game was up, and that within a matter of hours have posses closing down on all sides. Which meant that Hugh Taylor would be riding to the Tumbling T.

Or would he?

"Let's ride!" I said sharply. "He'll head for the T to see Mag, or I'm off my head. Or maybe to see me for a showdown. In any event, Keys and Kettle will want to see me, and from what I told them at the Horsethief Canyon, they'll know where to come. Let's go!"

Not waiting for Shorty to saddle, I threw a leg over Rowdy and lit out over that trail to the Tumbling T. That ride was one of the fastest I ever made on a horse, and Rowdy felt like running. We took off down the trail, skirting the cliffs until I could see the moonlight on the roofs at the T. The whole place was ablaze with lights, so I slowed down. Leaving Rowdy in the shadow of the stone stable, I moved up toward the house.

It was almost daylight, and the sky was growing gray. In the ranch yard were several horses, and I could see a dark group of them standing beyond the house, and several men were loitering about. Whoever was here was on the ground in force. On cat feet, I Injunned up to the house and slid in close to a window. Inside were several people. I could see Win Dolliver, his face dark and angry, and with him was Maggie. She was as pale as he was dark, and her eyes were wide.

"He's not here, and he hasn't been here in days!" Maggie was saying. "Now take your men, and get out!"

"He'll come here." That was Keys speaking. "He's gone soft on you. He told Hugh he was in love with you."

Her eyes went to Hugh. "He said that?" Her chin lifted. "Well, all right, then. I'm in love with him. "

My heart jumped, and I gripped the window sill hard. Yet Hugh was speaking now, and I listened.

"So? You sold me out, did you? You dropped me for an-oth-er man?"

She turned to him. "I'm sorry, Hugh. I was intending to tell you. I was never in love with you, and you know it. I liked you, yes. You persuaded me, and I listened, but I never felt sure about you, never liked the company you kept."

Bill Keys laughed harshly at that.

"And I hoped you'd change," Maggie continued. "You didn't. Then he came along, and from then on I knew there could never be anyone else."

"He beats me out of my ranch and out of my girl!" Hugh said bitterly. "That's a pretty thing!"

"I think you tried to rob him, Hugh," Maggie said, "and you tried to have him murdered!"

"I wish I had!" he complained bitterly.

"Boss," Keys interrupted, "let's get outside and get the boys set. If he's comin', he'll be here soon."

"Hugh," Maggie warned, "if you don't take your men and leave here at once, I'll hate you."

"Wouldn't that be awful," Keys sneered.

Hugh Taylor turned on him.

"Be still!" he said sharply. "I'll make the comments here!"

Keys's eyes narrowed angrily. "You'd better make 'em, then!" he snapped. "You've sure played hell with all your fancy figurin'. Mixin' this fancy doll into this has messed it up for sure. Take the boys, and light out of here. I'll take care of Mr. Wat Bell when he comes."

"You'd better get outside and wait until I come," Hugh said sharply. "I don't want any comments made about Miss Dolliver."

Bill Keys stared at Hugh, his eyes ugly with hatred. "Don't get high and mighty, Taber, or whatever your name is. We follered you because you figured things right and we made money. This deal looked good until you got to mixin' women with it, but don't think we can't get shut of you just as quick if we decide we want to."

Hugh Taylor turned on Keys. "Are you huntin' a showdown?" he demanded.

That was my cue to get away from that window.

In three long, silent jumps I made it to the back door and eased inside. I took it easy, and no more than a word or two could have passed before I was just inside the kitchen and could hear them in the next room. Keys was on the prod, I could see that.

"Showdown?" Keys was saying. "I reckon there wouldn't be no showdown betwixt you and me, Taber. If we're goin to kill Wat Bell, we'd better get outside. We can settle this later, but I'm tellin' you, don't go to givin' me orders. Not in that voice."

Hugh's voice was icy. "All right, Keys! Let's go outside!"

I knew that tone. I'd heard it before, and this was a showdown whether Keys wanted it or not. He had ridden some rough trails since I'd known him, Hugh had, but I doubted that he was gunslick enough to stack up right in a gun scrap with either Keys or Kettle.

Keys and Kettle went outside, and Hugh followed them.

In a quick step, I was into the room. Win wheeled at the sound of my movement, and Mag stood riveted where she was.

"Wat! Oh, you mustn't be found here! Go away!"

"Win, you take care of her!"

She had come right to my arms, and I was holding her close, looking over my shoulder at Dolliver.

"Get a shotgun … you've got one, I know. Get all your shells. If the worst comes to the worst, stand them off with that. I'm going out there!"

"You're a fool to do that, Wat," Win said seriously. "You won't have a chance, man!"

"No, I've got to side Hugh. They are going to kill him. He can't see it, either. He can't see that Keys wants a showdown. They've got the idea from him. Most of the work and planning is done, so now Keys and Kettle figure it's all over. They want to get rid of him."

"You'd side the man who tried to have you killed?" Win was incredulous.

I shrugged, knowing I was probably a fool.

"He's my cousin. We grew up like brothers, and Uncle Tom would have liked it that way. Anyway, those men out there are my enemies as well as his."

From the door I took a quick, careful look at the yard. This was it, all right. Keys had walked a dozen feet away from Hugh and turned to face him. Wolf Kettle had strolled off to the right, at least fifty feet from Keys. They made two corners with Hugh Taylor as the point of the triangle.

Keys spoke first. "Taber, we don't like this setup. We don't like you lordin' it over us … comin' high and mighty around. We don't like you takin' most of the money, either. We've decided to cut you out of the deal."

Maybe I'm cold-blooded, but I was curious. I wanted to see how much of the Bell blood there was in Hugh. For the first time in his life, so far as I knew, Hugh was called face to face, and if ever a man was called by a pair of curly wolves from the way back and rough, it was these two. What would he do? That was what I wondered.

For almost a half minute, he didn't say anything, but he must have been thinking plenty, and when he spoke, I could have cheered. The hombre may have tried to frame me, he may have hit the wrong trails, but he was my cousin.

"Why, sure, Bill," he said. "You do want a showdown, don't you? And you, Kettle? Sure there's more of the coyote in you than the wolf. This is what they called giving a man the Black Spot in a story I read once. Funny thing, it was a pirate story, and I read it with Wat … a better man than either of you."

He took a step closer toward them, his eyes shifting from one to the other.

"Spread wide, aren't you? Well, I'll take one of you to hell with me, anyway!"

Their hands were poised when I stepped out of the door. As I stepped out, I spoke.

"Which one do you want, Hugh? I'll take the other. I'm siding you."

Keys's eyes lifted to me, then Kettle's. They weren't happy about this change in the situation, not even a little bit. Hugh did not turn a hair.

"Take Kettle," he said, "Keys has been begging for it."

"There's a good bit of skunk in both of them," I said calmly. "Trot out your coyote, Kettle. You asked for it."

I hit the ground with a jump, digging in both heels and drawing as I landed.

Kettle flashed a fast gun, I'll say that for him, and he dropped into a crouch, snarling like the wolf he was named for. I saw his gun wink red, and then I was walking into him, triggering my right hand Colt.

Kettle fired and fired again, and then my second shot hit him just below the shirt pocket, and he lifted up on his tiptoes, and I slammed another one in for good measure. He went down, clawing at the dirt with both hands, and then I turned on my heel to see Hugh was down on his face but struggling to get up, and Keys was cursing viciously and trying to get a gun up for one more shot.

"Drop it, Bill!" I yelled. "Drop it or take it!"

The face he turned on me was a mask of viciousness. Down he might be, and badly wounded, but he was a cornered cougar at that moment, boiling with all his innate viciousness. His gun came up, and I felt the shock of the bullet, then the report. I got my balance and lifted my gun, then fired. The shot turned him around on his knee and dropped him, but he wouldn't die.

With a lunge, he got to his feet. His shirt was soaked with blood, and he stood there tottering and opened up on me with both guns. They turned into coughing, spitting flame, and I took another step straight forward and fired again, then shifted guns and slammed two more into him.

Still snarling, he took a step back, so full of lead he was top heavy, but he stood there, cursing wickedly and glaring at me. Then his eyes seemed to glaze over, and, mouthing curses, he went to the ground. I turned and took a look back at Kettle, but he was done for.

Looking up at the dark line of men near the horses, I told them: "This is it, boys. Drop your guns!"

They must have thought me completely crazy. I was hit once and maybe more, and my guns were almost empty, yet I was calling out twelve hardcase riders, all of them gun handlers.

"That's right!" It was Shorty Carver from the barn. "Let go your belts easy! We've got you covered!"

"I'm holding a shotgun, and there's plenty of shells!" Win chimed in from the house.

They hesitated, and I didn't blame them. There were a dozen of them, but they could see the rifle from the barn and the shotgun from the house. The rifle was a Spencer, firing a .56 caliber bullet of three hundred and sixty grains. It took no great imagination to realize that while some of them might, and probably would, get away, the Spencer would account for several, and a man hit with a .56 caliber bullet don't travel far. As for the shotgun, it had twin barrels, and that meant two dead men without reloading. As for me, I was tottering on my feet, but I'd missed only one shot of all I'd fired, and nobody wanted to gamble I'd miss more. It was a cinch anywhere from four to seven of them would hit dirt before the rest got away. And nobody was sure he wouldn't be one of the seven.

"To hell with it!"

The black mustached man who had recalled me from Sonora let go his belts, and it was a signal. They all did likewise.

At that moment a half-dozen riders swept down the hill and into the yard. Two of them wore badges. I turned and walked slowly toward Hugh as Win and Maggie rushed from the house toward me.

Dropping on one knee, I turned him over gently. His eyes flickered open, and he looked at me. There was nothing anybody could do for him. Bill Keys hadn't been missing any shots, and the only wonder was that Hugh was still alive.

"Thanks, kid," he whispered. "You were right on time. You

and Mag … I'm glad. Real glad." His breath sobbed in his lungs for three deep, agonized gasps, and then he spoke again. "Unc … le Tom … he told me why … left ranch … you. Knew I was … crook … I was a fool."

We got him inside then, and along about three that morning, he hung up his spurs.

In another room, I was having my own trouble, for I'd taken two slugs instead of one, and the Doc had to dig one of them out. It came hard, but I had a bullet to bite on while he probed for it. Mag was with me, with me all the time, although twice I sent her to see how Hugh was coming.

He came out of it, Hugh did, just before the end, and when he did, I got out of bed and went in. Doc told me I was crazy, but I went.

He looked up at me from the bed.

"It's all square, Hugh," I said, "tell Uncle Tom 'hello.'"

"You think I'll see him?" he asked me, and his voice was mighty hoarse.

"Sure you will," I said. "Any cowhand might take a wrong trail once or put the wrong brand on a cow. I think the Inspector up there can read your brand right."

"Thanks, kid," he said, "when you grew up, you sure grew tall."

I took his hand then, and he was looking up at me when his eyes blinked and his grip tightened, then loosened.

"He's all yours, boy," I said softly. "Let him have his head."

You know, I'll swear he smiled … it was really something, after all, to have a friend like Hugh.

THE END

ABOUT THE AUTHOR

Louis L'Amour was born in Jamestown, North Dakota in 1908. From his earliest youth, L'Amour had a love of verse. His first published work was a poem, "The Chap Worth While," appearing when he was eighteen years old in his former hometown's newspaper, the *Jamestown Sun*. L'Amour wrote poems and articles for a number of magazines through the early 1930s and, after many rejection slips, finally had his first story accepted, "Anything for a Pal" in *True Gang Life* (1935). In 1938 he joined his family where they had settled in Choctaw, Oklahoma, determined to make writing his career. "The Town No Guns Could Tame" in *New Western* (1940) was his first published Western story. L'Amour then agreed to write Western stories for the various Western pulp magazines published by Standard Magazines, a third of which appeared under the byline Jim Mayo. L'Amour's first Western novel under his own byline was *Westward the Tide* (1950). L'Amour sold his first Western short story to a slick magazine two years later, "The Gift of Cochise" in *Collier's* (1952). With *Showdown at Yellow Butte* (1953) by Jim Mayo, L'Amour began a series of short Western novels for Ace Publishing, but it was his association with Bantam Books for which he wrote the Sackett series and many other original paperbacks that made him a household name. He was the first American novelist to be awarded a National Gold Medal for his literary achievement.